Vampire Apocalypse

The Enoch Wars, Book 2

By Ben Settle

EnochWars.com

Ben Settle

CRYPT OF CONTENTS

"The progeny of the fallen angels with the daughters of Adam…are called in Gen. 6, Ne-phil-im, which means fallen ones (from naphal, to fall). What these beings were can be gathered only from Scripture. They were evidently great in size, as well as great in wickedness. They were superhuman, abnormal beings; and their destruction was necessary for the preservation of the human race, and for the faithfulness of Jehovah's Word (Gen. 3:15). This was why the Flood was brought 'upon the world of the ungodly' (2 Pet. 2:5) as prophesied by Enoch (Jude 14)."

- E.W. Bullinger
The Companion Bible, Appendix 25

Ben Settle

1
THE PLAYER

"Wow, these fellas really let themselves go."

-Tallahassee
Zombieland

- 1 -

"Put that fucking phone away!" said Azriel as he grabbed his date's new iPhone from her hand, slammed it on the table, and impaled it with his steak knife.

It'd been months since he lost control of his temper. And this time he assumed it had nothing to do with zombies. Or seeing pictures of his mother and girlfriend being raped by a sadistic zombie cop. Or recurring nightmares of the zombie cop's atrocities.

No, this time he assumed it was because of a woman.

But not just any woman.

It was a woman with terrible manners.

Her name was Mina, an attractive ("an 8.5 on a scale of 10," Azriel declared) woman he'd met online 6 months earlier.

"Omigod what the hell!" she said. There was a piece of spinach visibly stuck in her teeth.

"Learn some manners."

"Manners? You just broke my new phone!"

"Quiet," said Azriel tossing a wad of cash on the table and nodding at the waiter. As he pushed his chair out, he forgot to suck his ever-expanding gut in. His belly poked out enough where it forced his shirt to untuck itself, revealing his bare navel.

Mina, temporarily forgetting about her busted iPhone, giggled.

"I totes didn't realize you were getting this fat!" she laughed. Mina looked at her face in her compact mirror. "Why didn't you tell me there was food in my teeth asshole?"

"Let's go," said Azriel. He grabbed her hand and yanked the steak knife out of her phone.

Azriel couldn't wait to put Mina in a cab and send her home. She'd been growing steadily more bitchy, disrespectful, and hard to get along with for weeks no matter how much Azriel went out of his way to make her happy. She had also been hanging out with her new Tango instructor almost every night while insisting they were *"totes* just friends." And in the restaurant, after showing up 45-minutes late, she talked about the instructor and how rad he was for over an hour. The only time she stopped talking was to check her phone and respond to texts every time Azriel started speaking. Then, after she ate the $100 dinner Azriel was paying for and they were waiting for dessert, Mina — eyes stuck on her iPhone — informed Azriel she had to go, her friends were waiting for her at the club across town, and thanks, it's been an awesome six months, but I'm just not feeling a *connection* anymore, let's just be friends, k? — followed by a flirty giggle as she texted someone, not even looking Azriel in the eyes.

That's when Azriel snapped and busted her phone.

He couldn't help himself.

He'd been trying to control his violent temper in the three years since he killed the zombies and was usually successful. But something unusual was happening that night and he couldn't contain it. He had already felt antsy and increasingly paranoid – like he was being *watched* – while walking to the restaurant and didn't know why. He found it especially hard to keep his temper in check when he got to the restaurant. Mina's tardiness and disrespect was grating on him. He was suddenly realizing how repulsive and unattractive her personality was. And when she started responding to texts while he was talking, he felt an overwhelming urge either to stab her or the phone that she was glued to.

He chose the phone.

However, Azriel couldn't blame her for laughing at his belly. He had gained a lot of weight in his stomach, while his legs and arms were still skinny. This was a result of a year of near-daily binge drinking and eating (Hot Tamales candy and LandShark lager being his favorite vices), and sitting in a chair for 8, 9, even 10 hours per day writing advertising as a freelance copywriter. He tried motivating himself to exercise. Tried eating better. Tried eating less. But it was no use. His appetite for sweet foods and beer was as hot as his temper. And he figured he'd simply learn to live with getting winded just walking up and down stairs, having to hold his breath to tie his shoes, and creatively layering his clothes and sucking in his gut to hide his mass.

And why not?

Who did he have to be in shape for?

These low class bitches he met online?

Most of them either didn't look anything like their photos, or had such flawed personalities and emotional damage they were barely worthy of what his late friend Marvin Worley would call a "pump & dump."

Azriel didn't think he needed to stay in shape for survival reasons, either.

What about the monsters Pastor Shane and Finius said would seek him out?

Where were they?

Three years and not so much as a twitch in that internal alarm in his gut that alerted him whenever he was around monsters.

So he stopped caring or worrying about them.

The only thing he was concerned about was his temper. That vicious, scary, violent temper that made him as damaged as the girls he dated.

And, he did.

He had his outbursts and arguments with Mina in public.

But nothing that attracted too much attention.

That is, until he destroyed Mina's phone and the restaurant fell silent.

Azriel was confused. Yes, she was acting like a stuck up bitch. But why did he feel an almost uncontrollable urge to kill?

Why were his violent instincts kicking in now of all times?

- 2 -

"You douche bag that phone was new! My gay friend at Apple gave it to me and paid like... a *lot* for it!" said Mina. Azriel found it amusing how she always emphasized her "gay" friend. Not just a friend. No, it was her *gay* friend. And she always said it in a tone that sounded as if she was bragging about an exotic pet.

Azriel marched Mina towards the nearest empty cabstand. It was 9:45 p.m. and the moon was full and so bright that it shed more light on them than the streetlights did. The newly constructed Fenris Tower loomed in the horizon. It had been finished a year earlier, and was controversial because it dwarfed the Sears Tower's height and altered the historical Chicago skyline.

"I don't tolerate low class jackass behavior," said Azriel, sitting on a bench, undoing his belt, and letting his flabby stomach poke out.

Screw it, he thought, *she just said it's over with us anyway.*

"You're so buying me a new phone," said Mina sitting next to him and suppressing a smile. Since leaving the restaurant she found Azriel suddenly more attractive than ever – even as she told herself she was furious with him for breaking her iPhone.

"No."

"What do you mean 'no'! I thought you were really rad before. What happened to you? You think you're like such a player don't you... that you can just act like a jerk and girls like it. It doesn't work on me, mister."

"Shut up..." said Azriel sitting up straight and scanning his surroundings. Even though he had lived a sedentary life the past year especially after dumping Finius and the zombie head in the Belasco quicksand pit, his Predator instincts – bred and honed through thousands of years of genetic manipulation – were as strong as ever. He was starting to suspect his temper flare up was not just about the girl, after all. It was something else and Mina just happened to be there when it happened. He pulled a small bag of Hot Tamales candy out of his sport coat pocket, ripped it open with his teeth, and poured the entire bag into his mouth.

His cheeks poked out from all the candy and he slowly chewed as Mina prattled on about how she had never been treated like this before and he'd have to really work hard if he ever expected her to talk to him again.

As Azriel chewed the candy, he tuned her annoying voice out.

He also tuned out the delicious cinnamon taste he loved so much.

He even tuned out the cab that drove by that he could have hailed.

No, he was focusing on something else:

A feeling that some thing was nearby.

- 3 -

"We have to go," said Azriel as he grabbed Mina's wrist.

Fuck! I should have hailed that cab, he thought, not even bothering to edit his thoughts. For professional reasons, he was trying to not reflexively swear – audibly, or in his mind – anymore, and usually substituted the word "Balls!" for "Fuck!" It amused his clients, and made him more likable. But something was not right and not swearing was the last thing on his mind.

Azriel's grip shocked Mina. She knew he was a lot stronger than he looked. It was one of the things that originally attracted her to him. But if he squeezed any harder it felt like he'd break a bone. It hurt her, but turned her on too. Not that she was going to let him know that.

"Go where?" asked Mina. "Why didn't you grab that cab? And don't think you're not buying *me* a new phone –"

Azriel wheeled Mina around in front of him and put his hand over her mouth. "Shut up. We're being followed. Understand?" Azriel waited for her to nod before letting her turn her gaze away. His eyes slightly glowed red, but she didn't seem to notice. She was so insulted by him shushing her, and yet so turned on by his aggressiveness, she didn't know if she wanted to punch him or jump his bones. A thought – more a *hope* – raced through her head that maybe... just *maybe*... she'd get to do both before the night ended.

Azriel led Mina down the sidewalk.

There were no other people around and his first thought was to find a crowd to blend in to. His urge to break something... to *kill* something... grew stronger every second. He hadn't felt anything like it since the zombies.

Azriel saw some people three blocks away at a corner and decided to take her there. Then he would lead whoever – or *what* ever – was following them away, where he could deal with it. He thought back to Pastor Shane saying monsters would sense Azriel and want to kill him, and how Azriel would sense them and want to kill them. That seemed like thirty years ago, not three. And the whole time since dumping Chief Rawger, Finius, and the original zombie head into the quicksand pit in Belasco, Azriel wondered if anyone would find him.

If anything, he had felt safer than ever.

His little copywriting business exploded with clients and money. He was living like a king in a nice apartment, with no wife or kids to pay for and no car or house note. He had lots of cash, no debt, and started partying a lot, living like a player on a roll. If anyone had lived after he destroyed Belasco, nobody would recognize his puffy face and fat gut anyway.

Azriel liked eating and drinking... and partying... and women.

Oh, how he loved women.

His whole life he'd been a skinny outcast and couldn't have gotten a date with a pocket full of $50's. But since discovering his true nature, what he was *capable* of... and achieving a certain level of financial and professional success, getting dates was easy – on the Internet, at least. The hard part was keeping them. His six months with Mina was the longest relationship he'd had. And as annoying as she was, he was starting to really like her. Part of it was her huge breasts. But it was also because in his own way, he knew he was as damaged as she was and they took comfort in each other's imperfections.

Azriel was getting even antsier.

Where was this thing following him?

Was it invisible?

Some kind of monster he couldn't see?

And if it was going to jump them before he got her to safety, would it just *do* it already so he could kick its ass?

Azriel rushed Mina past a dark alley. As they walked by the entrance several pairs of strong hands grabbed his ankles and yanked him into the blackness. The same happened to Mina. A white hand with long fingernails also covered her mouth to stifle her scream.

- 4 -

Azriel kicked and flailed his arms and legs as though he were drowning.

His night vision came into focus. But he couldn't tell how many there were... or even *what* they were. They were all dressed in nice pants and jackets. Their hands had unusually long fingernails and he saw sharp top row teeth protruding out of some of their mouths that went as far down their faces as their chins.

Vampires? Has to be!

Azriel had only seen one vampire – and that was in a photo in Pastor

13

Shane's house of the tall vampire who founded Belasco, Illinois. It wore a nice suit and top hat, holding a severed woman's head while smiling for the camera. The mere thought of that photo enraged Azriel, as did his new attackers' presence.

The vampires pinned Azriel down. They smelled his face and neck, hissing and speaking words he couldn't understand. Azriel figured they were probably as averse to wanting to drink his blood as the zombies were to eating his flesh. He couldn't see Mina, but he assumed they were already either feasting on her, or preparing to.

Azriel instinctively head butted the vampire on top of him.

The head butt's force smashed into the vampire's head like a bowling ball.

The vampire reeled back.

Blood streamed out of its nose.

Azriel looked to his right and another vampire's face was next to his – hissing. Its breath smelled like a dead skunk. Azriel bit down on its nose. More blood sprayed as it slunk off him, loosening his right arm, which he used to grab the vampire on his left's neck, and squeezed the neck as hard as he could.

Azriel spat out the blood that got into his mouth from the bite. The bitter taste replaced the sweet hot tamales taste in his mouth.

He heard a cracking sound as he broke the vampire's neck.

He sat up and scanned the alley.

It was packed with vampires.

There were at least a dozen of them.

He noticed two vampires on their knees, hovering over Mina. Her throat was torn to ribbons. Blood sprayed out of her jugular like a fountain into their smiling, fanged faces.

- 5 -

Azriel rushed the vampires feasting on Mina's neck.

He tackled the one on her right with his right arm, while grabbing the neck of the one on the left with his other hand, bringing the vampire down with him, crushing its throat in the process. Azriel didn't know if breaking a vampire's neck would kill it or how much pain they felt. He'd only seen the movies. And he assumed that, like with the zombies, what was in the movies was probably not 100% accurate. The vampire whose throat he crushed struggled to breathe and retreated towards the wall. The other one had already slipped out of Azriel's arm hold and was on its feet.

"Come on you sons of bitches!" panted Azriel, slowly standing up. "Bring it!"

Azriel was angry but tired, and wheezing like an asthmatic. His hands were on his knees, his back slightly bent over. He looked like a stiff wind could knock him down. The vampire closest to him threw back its head and laughed while the other vampires slunk up along beside and behind him.

The vampires encircled him and closed off his escape.

"We're disappointed in you," said the laughing vampire. "The *Skipper* said you'd put up a lot more fight than this. Look at you. You can barely stand!"

The vampires laughed.

Azriel hadn't felt this winded – *holy balls I think I'm gonna puke!* – since he was on the blue pills that made him feel sick and in pain whenever he even so much as *thought* about violence.

C'mon idiot !

Think!

Do something...

The vampires leapt at him and dog piled on top of him.

He could see nothing or think of anything to do.

As the vampire pile got taller and heavier, he found it hard to breathe.

He started to panic – not realizing until then he was claustrophobic. The rage he'd hoped would rescue him was nowhere to be found. He felt like he was drowning in a pool of bad breath and undead stench.

They smelled just like the zombies.

Balls!

- 6 -

Azriel heard that when you are dying, you see your whole life flash before your eyes. But as he started to lose consciousness from the vampires killing him in one of the only ways he *could* be killed... suffocation... he could only think about what an ass hat he'd been to let himself get so out of shape.

To get so lazy.

To get so *weak*.

Use the switch, Dumb Az!, he snapped at himself.

It'd been months since he called himself that. And it'd been even longer since he thought about that mental switch in his brain that let him control the zombies' minds, letting him lead them to their deaths like rats following the Pied Piper. Maybe it'd let him control these vampires, too, he thought, as he flipped the switch up and down.

Nothing.

He tried it again.

This time one of the vampires right on top of him gasped, not in pain, but surprise.

That was weird, thought Azriel.

He pushed the switch again, focusing on the same vampire.

The vampire disappeared.

No, it didn't disappear, Azriel realized.

It *transformed*.

Azriel heard leathery wings flapping and caught a brief glimpse through a crack in the pile on top of him of a bat hovering above them. Then it immediately turned back into its regular vampire form, naked and startled. Whatever mechanism gave him the ability to seize a zombie's mind clearly did not work the same on these vampires. Nor even all the vampires.

Turn one of them into a bat?

Seriously?

That's all I got?

Azriel pushed the switch again.

Nothing happened.

Balls!

Think, idiot!

Pastor Shane told Azriel his body was hard to kill, but he could be killed under the right circumstances. When Todd Rawger beat him and buried him he didn't die. But he did remember slowly suffocating, and barely escaping his dirt grave before running out of air. Somehow these vampires knew that was one way to stop him. They seemed uninterested in trying to bite him, cut him, hit him, or damage him. Just suffocate him.

Azriel kept pushing that mental switch in his mind thinking maybe if he turned enough of them into bats he could at least escape the pile.

But nothing happened.

He felt himself losing consciousness.

There was nothing else he could do.

He prepared himself to die – a fat, wheezing sack of flesh.

Just like the rest of America, he thought.

Then came a muffled cackling noise from outside the vampire pile on top of him. The laugh reminded him of the Crypt Keeper on the old TV show *Tales From the Crypt*. The pressure on his body lessened. Air found its way into his lungs again.

- 7 -

As the weight of the vampire dog pile lessened, the Crypt Keeper laugh got louder, and Azriel could make out the cackler's words.

"Get up little Azriel, get up! Help me fight these limp-dicked fuck suckers!" it said.

It sounded like a lady's voice.

An *old* lady.

Azriel heard the wet sounds that flesh makes as it's being pounded. He heard hisses and screams and what sounded like a fist hitting bone. As the vampires faced their new attacker and let him up, he saw a small, gangly-looking fist come out of the vampire's back standing in front of him. Azriel couldn't see the attacker. All he saw was an old hand holding a slowly beating heart come through the vampire's back.

The vampire slumped to the ground revealing who the attacking cackler was:

A short and old (*old? No, ancient !* Azriel thought) lady with no eyelids.

She couldn't have been more than 5-feet tall and she looked almost like a cadaver. Her buggy eyes looked right through him. They reminded Azriel of Ralph Kramden's eyes from the *Honeymooners* TV show. She looked like a photo of the world's oldest living woman – only 100-years *older*, and more fragile and decrepit. There was a heart in her hand and a dead vampire at her feet.

"My but you *are* a cutie!" she said. "Watch out!"

Azriel was tackled to the ground by another vampire. It pounded on his face with its fists. Azriel hooked his thumb into the vampire's mouth – the "fish hook" move he'd seen a million times on the old martial arts movies he loved to watch – and pulled it by the cheek off him.

Azriel jumped to his feet and kicked it in the head.

Its skull caved in from the impact.

Azriel was so winded he felt like he'd just run a marathon. The large meal he'd had and that whole bag of Hot Tamales candy he ate festered in his belly – bloating him up – and he just wanted to burp.

"You pussy!" said the old lady as she had one of the vampires in a chokehold. She lifted up with her arms and effortlessly twisted the vampire's head clean off. There was a loud ripping noise as she detached the vampire's head from its spine. Its body slunk to the ground. She held the head up for Azriel to see, like a child looking for his approval, as if she was saying, "*See what I can do? Did you see?*"

The vampire on Azriel was choking him and didn't see the old lady come up behind him until it was too late. She punched a hole right through its back and yanked its heart out as she did to the other vampires she killed.

The vampire fell to the ground.

Its arms and legs still twitched.

"Who are you?" panted Azriel. He was breathing so hard he felt his heart was going to beat right out of his chest as efficiently as the old lady pulled out the vampire's heart at his feet.

"Boy you are dumb. Dumb! I should have let them *kill* you! You're as useless as my saggy titties and my dried, barren cunt!"

Another round of cackling.

Azriel couldn't tell if she was angry or simply amusing herself.

"Let's look at you..." she said, leering at Azriel with her lidless eyes. "You've gotten fat, too, haven't you? Fat and useless and stupid. But I got need of you. You're a major player in this game and you've been sitting on the bench far too long. Time to suit up and play with the rest of us!"

She tossed the heart at Azriel.

He reflexively caught it, and then dropped it out of disgust.

It was still slowly beating.

"What are you talking about," said Azriel. Drool was coming out of his mouth from breathing so hard. His ribs hurt with every breath. "Who *are* you?

"Don't you see the resemblance? It's me. You're ever lovin' *Granny*. Now come here, give the 'nanna a big sloppy *kiss!*" she said, as she licked her old, pursed lips and puckered her face, darting her tongue out at him.

That's just fucking gross, thought Azriel.

2
FEZZIWIG

*"I'd give four million dollars just to be able to
take a piss without it hurting."*

- Hyman Roth
The Godfather 2

- 1 -

"Okay Concubine. I'm ready. Get up there good and *deep*," said the vampire Anghel "Fezziwig" Belasco, as his concubine named Starr prepared to give him a prostate massage. Fezziwig was on his side on the bed, his six-fingered hands pressed flat on the sheet, his cheek resting against the pillow.

"You know I always take care of you, Master," said Starr snapping a rubber glove on.

Starr was a beautiful, 24-year old woman who lived with Fezziwig in his Alaskan cottage outside of a small town called Bramstoke.

"Thank the LORD, this will feel so good..." moaned the vampire.

"There Master, how is that?" said Starr, massaging Fezziwig's softball-sized prostate.

"Better... much, much better. Now... *milk* it..."

"Yes, Master."

Over the past 60 years Fezziwig's prostate had started to give him trouble. Even when he could sustain a boner long enough to bed his young concubines, he felt an agonizing pin-prick pain when he ejaculated. And the constant urge to piss – all the time – was maddening. As soon as he sat down to watch another exciting episode of *Miami Vice* season 4 or his favorite movie *Men At Work*, he suddenly had to piss. Every time. Without exception. It was a sudden, uncontrollable urge that felt like he was going to go in his pants. It was so intense he usually thought he would not be able to even get to the bathroom in time. So he'd jump up, shuffle over to the toilet, and stand over the bowl for several minutes, with nothing coming out but a few drops from his wrinkled, flaccid penis. It was frustrating and painful. And he'd usually moan and yell and pound the wall with his fist next to the toilet.

Fezziwig was on multiple prostate drugs. But the only thing that gave him a little relief were Starr's prostate massages, during which he enjoyed lecturing her all about how much being a vampire sucked at his age.

How it hurt to piss.

How it hurt to shit.

How it hurt to have sex.

Even how it hurt his back to sit in his chair watching TV for more than 10 or 15 minutes at a time.

He had over a dozen other health problems that would flare up if he drank anything but Type A negative blood: Like diarrhea. Hemorrhoids. An itching, bleeding rash on his butt crack. Flaking skin on his eyelids kept falling into his eyeballs. And the list went on.

It was the ultimate paradox:

He was always in pain, yet he couldn't die.

If he was cut or hurt in a fight, or wounded, those would heal quickly and efficiently. But that wasn't the case with his internal body parts. He just kept living as his organs and nerves got inflamed and diseased. He often fantasized about the good old days when he was younger. He was still mostly as *strong* as he was back then. Still just as fast when he needed to be (but would *feel* it the next day if he got too crazy, and be sore for weeks after). And had mostly just as much energy. But there weren't any prostate problems or blood intolerances or other old man aches and pains back then.

But that was a long time ago.

And he accepted the fact those days weren't coming back.

Fezziwig (he preferred that name over his given name "Anghel") knew he was the oldest living being on the planet. He'd been around for thousands of years and had seen a lot of history unfold.

He witnessed the birth (and death) of Jesus Christ.

He fought in the Babylonian, Persian, Greek, Roman, and Eastern European wars.

Fezziwig had even watched the waters rise when Noah and his family boarded the ark. He still didn't know why he was allowed to live through that flood. But the LORD told him what to do to escape it, and he listened, and was still alive after everyone else he knew had drowned.

Fezziwig had lived a long life, but also a painful one. Especially as the world became more industrialized, and as toxins and poisons and chemicals brought on more diseases, cancers, and other ailments. It took just half a century for his body to break down and start developing health conditions nobody had even *heard* of in his younger days.

And now, as he got his regular prostate massage from Starr, he wished someone would just kill him and put him out of his misery.

Where is a Predator when you need one?

No, he couldn't count on anyone else to do it.

He'd have to do it himself and he would do it soon.

He'd already been making preparations for suicide in his mind for months. Including how to do it in the least painful way possible. Yes, he had it all planned out, he thought, as a fanged smile formed on his face. Until, as he lay there, Starr massaging away, lost in the suicide fantasy, the voice – *his* voice – came again, for the first time in three weeks.

"Starr, stop!" said Fezziwig.

"What is it, Master?"

"The LORD is speaking to me again. Shut up!"

- 2 -

Three weeks earlier, when Fezziwig heard the LORD's voice talking to him for the first time in more than 300 years, he dismissed it as yet another old man's disease. His body was falling apart – but wouldn't die. So he figured now maybe his mind was going, too.

Or maybe he was going senile?

Or getting Alzheimer's Disease?

Or was Schitzo?

Fezziwig chose this particular part of the world to live because it was dark a lot during certain times of the year, allowing him to move around more freely without risk of being cooked from the inside out by the sun. There was only one doctor – an old drunk named Dr. Schumacher – but he was scared of Fezziwig and refused to see him. But no matter, Fezziwig figured the doctor would simply say hearing voices was something that comes with age and to not worry about it.

So Fezziwig did what he thought the doctor would tell him, and went back to his life as usual.

Maybe he hadn't heard the LORD's voice after all.

And if that's the case, he could continue to mastermind his suicide.

Before then, a typical day for him involved yelling at Starr for any reason and no reason (he had a nasty temper, even for a vampire, and the older and more in pain he was, the *worse* it got). And then spending hours in front of his old 1975 TV set with the tube about ready to go, watching VHS tapes of *Men At Work* and *Miami Vice* season 4 ("it's the most *misunderstood* season," he would explain to Starr – each time telling it to her as if it was the first time he'd ever told her – such was his memory loss). He particularly enjoyed watching his VHS tapes while sipping on a glass of gin mixed with type A negative blood, which he sent Starr to get from the hospitals and blood banks regularly. Sometimes it would take her weeks to find any blood at all and he'd have to go with another blood type, flaring up all his food intolerance symptoms. He often found it easier and more stable to just take meds to mask the symptoms that Starr would also steal for him.

When he got tired of watching TV, he listened to talk radio. His favorite host was Michael Savage, even though Savage was still way too liberal for his tastes.

But what was an old vampire to do?

His entertainment options living in the woods were limited. Living there was a small price to pay to keep himself away from the attention of all the things that wanted to not just kill him – but *torture* him first. Old Fezziwig had racked up quite a list of enemies in his 5,500 years on the planet. And as far as he was concerned, they could all go fuck themselves.

He was too old to fight these faggots anymore.

Or, maybe he was just not as interested as he used to be.

He just wanted to die – but not at the hands of these faggot monsters and Predators. The Predators were especially bad. They had no honor. No sense of *pride* in their work. It was just "see monster, kill monster" – including the ones like him who kept out of trouble and had no desire to menace the world. Even the *bounty hunter* Predators seeking him out lacked any kind of discipline. Over the past few decades the U.S. government had started hiring Predators to capture monsters. Fezziwig was most frightened of those Predators in particular. What was the government doing with monsters if they weren't killing them? Experimenting on them? Dissecting them? Cutting them open to see what made them *tick*?

Fezziwig had no desire to find out.

Humans, in some cases, were more amoral than even some of his Nephilim kind were. It especially astonished and revolted him how humans butchered their own unborn children. Not even the most revolting of monsters – with the exception of the zombies and the dreaded tarasque – destroys their own children. It reminded Fezziwig of when Baal worshipers he knew in the ancient days sacrificed their young children into giant fires for personal convenience, crops, and gain. It amused Fezziwig how Baal -- who was merely a fallen angel, and not a "god" -- suckered those dumb faggots into worshiping him, when the entity had zero power to help them at all, nor would bother even if he did.

And on this day three weeks before the LORD spoke to Fezziwig again during his prostate massage, as luck (the bad kind – which was the only kind Fezziwig seemed to get) would have it, Fezziwig finally figured out a way to kill himself. It's difficult for vampires to commit suicide without it being painful. But, as he was standing over the toilet, desperate to squeeze even a few drops of piss out, he thought up a solution. And he was excited to do it. That is, until the voice of the LORD spoke to him for the first time since he founded Belasco, Illinois.

The voice was audible.

At least, he *thought* it was.

Or, maybe it was just an old man's senile mind playing tricks?

The only thing the LORD told Fezziwig, after a few hundred years of silence, was that he was *needed*.

And that was it.

"Needed for what?" Fezziwig yelled at his bathroom's blank wall.

There was no *physical* presence talking to him.

It was just a voice.

He later asked Starr if she'd heard the voice, too, from the bathroom, and she was slow to answer. She had heard nothing but was too scared of angering him. She wanted Fezziwig to fulfill on his promise to her. He promised to make her into an immortal vampire like him. But she never realized he had no damn intention of doing it. It was all just *pillow talk* as far as he was concerned. Fezziwig had discovered that the promise of eternal beauty was every hot woman's Achilles heel these days. The billion dollar cosmetic surgery industry took advantage of this fact, so why not Fezziwig, too? The allure of keeping them young and beautiful kept his concubines loyal and obedient and wanting to please him. But while Starr wanted to lie to appease him and say, *"Yes, Master, I heard it...,"* she knew she could easily be caught in that lie and punished. So at the risk of displeasing her Master with bad news, she shook her head and went back to work, compounding his various medicines for his myriad of health problems. For decades, Fezziwig had always seduced medical students into being his concubines. He needed a concubine who could mix his own medicines at home, because he didn't like dealing with pharmacists. And since Dr. Schumacher feared him, Fezziwig couldn't get his prescriptions even if there was a local pharmacy.

Starr may not have heard the LORD's voice, but Fezziwig heard it clearly: The LORD said he needed Fezziwig's help and time was short.

And that was it.

"But what do you want me to do?" Fezziwig would call out at odd times whenever he thought about that voice. And every time he did, he was met with silence.

It was odd.

Why wouldn't the LORD be clear with him?

Why not just tell him what he wanted?

Three weeks passed without hearing the LORD's voice. During that time Fezziwig decided yes, he was just going senile. He'd already started having more memory lapses – forgetting Starr's name (or calling her by any one of the dozens of his past concubines' names), or forgetting the name of Charlie Sheen's character in *Men At Work*, or not recognizing Don Johnson in *Miami Vice* season 4. (*Who is this faggot with the gay facial scruff? A new character?*) This didn't happen all the time – maybe once every few days, and usually only for a few minutes. But it happened enough where he didn't trust his own mind anymore.

And that's when Fezziwig got the idea to kill himself.

What is the point of living anymore?

He was always in pain.

He was losing his mind.

And lots of things wanted him dead anyway, including the terrifying monster he had locked away in the basement that could demolish an entire state in a matter of days. Fezziwig often cursed the Predator and faggot cleric who saddled him with that babysitting responsibility more than 800 years earlier.

Worst of all, his greatest pleasures – watching TV and listening to talk radio – was starting to bore him. Or maybe he was just frustrated his old VHS deck was having tracking problems and the tapes made an annoying screeching sound.

Either way, life was sucking more than ever before.

Why put off the sweet release of death any longer?

- 4 -

The plan to kill himself was a simple one:

The only way to kill a vampire besides sunlight or dousing it with holy water, was to stake it through the heart, cut off its head, stuff the mouth with garlic, and burn the body.

It was an impossible task to do to by himself even under the best of circumstances.

Fezziwig needed help.

And that's where Starr came in.

The problem was, he promised her he would turn her into a vampire at "the appointed time" while telling her some bullshit lie about how it had to be under a blood red moon in the middle of the summer. But she was a naive girl (he always targeted the naive ones), as well as loyal and submissive and obedient – the way Fezziwig liked all his concubines.

"Will you turn me before you die?" asked Starr when Fezziwig told her his plan to kill himself.

She didn't really care so much that he wanted to die. She understood his reasons. She was the one who had to give him sponge baths, prostate massages, and cleaned his bedpan every day while he sat there farting and groaning and shouting at her and the TV. Fezziwig also sent her down into the basement each day to make sure the monster he was babysitting was still asleep. The way he figured, better her to be eaten alive than him. Her screams would give him enough time to turn into a bat and flee, assuming it wasn't daylight out. Starr had spent the last two years with Fezziwig enduring this – in a town that could have been the asshole of the universe (*or within crapping distance of it*, as Fezziwig would say) for all she knew. She put up with being Fezziwig's bitch, listening to him verbally abuse her at every chance, throwing blood bags at her if he didn't like the taste, and putting up with his constant complaining about his health, world politics, and all the goddamn faggot liberals running the world... and how back in his day guys like Genghis Kahn would have had these fudge packer leaders publicly flogged and executed. Fezziwig especially had an unusual love for lecturing her. He enjoyed listening to the sound of his own voice. He relished talking for hours at a time, explaining what he was thinking about any subject on his mind, in as much detail as possible.

When Starr asked about turning her, he had to think quickly. And like the Grinch in the old story books, he thought up a great lie on the spot:

"When I'm dead, you can simply drink my blood and you'll become a vampire, too, Concubine. Dead vampire blood turns humans into vampires. That's the *secret*."

Of course, that was a lie.

Drinking the blood of a *dead* vampire wouldn't turn her into a vampire any more than drinking the blood of a dead mouse would turn her into a mouse.

But she didn't need to know that, did she?

And so, after a few days of prep, they had everything in place.

She would give Fezziwig a massive dose of Vicodin and put an entire bottle of red wine directly into his body via a catheter in his jugular vein, so he'd be unconscious. Then, she would behead him, stuff garlic in his mouth, stake him through the heart, toss his body in the burn can out back, and then set it on fire.

"Ready, Master?" asked Starr. She handed Fezziwig the entire bottle of Vicodin with a goblet of Type A *positive* blood. That particular blood always tasted so good... but would have him hunched over in stomach pain for hours if he drank a single drop. However, since he was going to die anyway he figured why not? It'd be like giving a dying celiac his last damn piece of glutinous homemade *bread*.

"Yes, concubine," he snapped. "I am ready. *Hurry*."

But as Fezziwig lifted his old hand to his mouth to dump the bottle of Vicodins down his throat, while Starr was about to inject his body with an entire bottle of red wine... he heard the voice of the LORD again.

- 5 -

"*Don't!*" screamed the voice of the LORD.

Fezziwig howled in disgust. He shook his arms up and down in frustration like an obnoxious kid who didn't get his way.

Why is it *now* of all times he had to hear that goddamn voice again?

It didn't seem like anything went right for Fezziwig. It was almost like bad luck followed him around. Now the miserable old vampire couldn't even kill himself. Not with the voice of the LORD commanding him to stop at the last second.

"Why are you doing this to me!" said Fezziwig at the ceiling.

Starr looked at him blankly.

Now who was this old fool talking to?

The voice of the LORD said: "Go to Belasco. Go *home.*"

Fezziwig hated that town.

When he heard about the explosion in the woods three years earlier, and how the whole town's population was mysteriously wiped out, he laughed. He'd built that town for a very specific reason. And after that reason was fulfilled, he left only to return to check on it every few decades, letting the citizens kill each other, fuck each other, and do whatever other dark and evil things they wanted to do to each other. His work there was over. He wanted to hide from the Predators and other monsters always wanting to attack, fight, or torture him.

Fezziwig didn't want to be hunted down anymore.

He wanted to be left the hell alone.

That town was pure evil.

It attracted evil things.

Many of those evil things hated Fezziwig.

Plus, there was a rumor that a new Predator had been raised there. An unusually powerful one. Fezziwig wanted nothing to do with the Predators. He'd fought and killed a few in his time, and he hated the way they fought "dirty."

Fezziwig wanted to forget all about Belasco.

But the LORD was commanding him to go.

But why? Why did he have to go?

The LORD had no answer the day he interrupted Fezziwig's suicide. But it was clear he wasn't just going crazy this time. The voice was even clearer, as if the LORD was standing right next to him speaking in his ear.

So Fezziwig would go to Belasco, Illinois.

But, he had to be prepared.

If the LORD wanted him there, there must be a damn good reason for it.

And he'd be ready for whatever that reason was.

- 6 -

The first thing Fezziwig had to do was make preparations.

Traveling was delicate for him at best. If he wanted to travel, he had to be careful due to sunlight.

Thus, it was time to make the concubine useful again.

He needed another lie to string her along ("Why are you leaving Master?") so she would expect him to return and be eager to help him get going. This time he told her a lie saying he was going to get some things from Belasco to turn her into a vampire and he needed her help. And like the native concubine Starr was, she didn't question him and was indeed eager to help. She took care of all the arrangements. He would fly out of the airport that was an hour's drive away on the red eye and fly into O'Hare Airport well before dawn. He would have to find a place to hole up in the city, then travel to Belasco which he would do as a bat at night. He liked his bat form – what he called being "bat mobile." He could travel farther and faster that way than on foot. Although being bat mobile was not always a safe way to travel, due to the high population of owls who liked to eat bats.

But, if everything went according to plan, he would be in Belasco in a few days. The only question was this: Just what was he supposed to do when he got there? The voice of the LORD didn't say. And no matter how much Fezziwig called out to the LORD, the LORD did not answer.

That is, until the day before he was set to depart, while Starr gave Fezziwig his prostate massage.

The voice of the LORD spoke to him once again.

And this time it told him to listen very carefully...

- 7 -

When the voice of the LORD gave Fezziwig his marching orders, Fezziwig was confused.

The orders didn't make a whole lot of sense.

He wondered how he would pull it off alone.

And as if the voice of the LORD had anticipated this question, it gave him the answer:

The Chosen Predator – Lucifer's *favorite* – is returning to Belasco. It was the same Predator who killed the zombies and wiped out the entire town three years earlier. Fezziwig had heard about those events through the dark channels who gave him news of his town's status.

Everyone died.

Every single soul was gone.

This Predator was especially powerful, and Fezziwig would need his help to accomplish the LORD's plan.

But wouldn't the Predator want to kill him?

Of course he would.

And that was Fezziwig's hardest challenge: Convincing the Predator – who he knew would hate him on sight, as all Predators *instinctively* do – to help.

The LORD was right.

Fezziwig would need someone with strength like the Predator to pull off his mission.

"But how do you know he'll be there?" Fezziwig asked.

"He's already on his way," said the voice of the LORD.

3

MONSTER MASSACRE

*"Yea, though I walk through the valley of the shadow of death I shall fear no evil,
because I am the meanest son-of-a-bitch in the valley."*

- Author Unknown
Properly Attributed to General Patton

- 1 -

"We gotta clean these butt-suckers up lickety split," said Granny, peering around the alley with her giant lidless eyeballs. She still had a vampire heart in her hand.

"It's still beating…?" said Azriel.

"When those pricks from The Order *stole* you from me I knew you'd grow up to be a bitch. They didn't tell you jack titty did they?"

"I don't have time for this. Who are you, really," said Azriel.

"You haven't seen me since you were a teeny tiny baby. Just call me Granny though, k? Never mind your other questions for now, Porky. We got to take care of these vamps." Azriel noticed she only had a few teeth left, and words she said with the letter "s" in them sounded like whistles.

Azriel didn't know if he believed she was his grandma or not. But if she were, then Azriel could only assume whatever it was in their Predator genetics that made them hard to kill also included being hard to kill by *age*, too. She looked like she was a couple hundred years old. But she was as fast, strong, and tough as he was.

It all seemed impossible.

Then again, so were the things he'd seen and done, too.

"We gotta dispose of them proper, see?" said Granny. She walked to the wall where there was a large backpack she'd brought, and pulled a couple wooden stakes out. "Quickly now, we have to stake every one of them through the heart before they start coming back to life. Understand?"

Within minutes, they had staked all the dead vampires through the hearts – including the hearts Granny pulled out of chests with her bare hands – and proceeded to behead them, stuff their mouths with garlic cloves from Granny's backpack, and toss them in a big dumpster. Granny lit a match by scratching it on one of her remaining teeth, then set the dumpster's contents on fire.

Azriel looked out for pedestrians.

He wondered how long they had been in the alley?

Minutes ?

Hours?

More like *seconds*, he realized. The whole fight was fast.

They watched the vampire bodies burn up. The fire had an unusual bluish color, not the orange or yellow one would expect. Azriel wondered if anyone walking by that alley would notice the bizarrely-colored fire, but nobody passed by.

Before he started letting the life of partying and drinking and chasing girls get the best of him, Azriel would, at rare and odd times, feel like someone... or some *thing*... was watching him. When it happened it made him paranoid, and he'd have nightmares of Chief Rawger standing over his bed, with his zombified friends Marvin Worley and Kerri Ditzler standing there with him, all feasting on his genitals as he screamed how sorry he was. Those dreams seemed so real. But then something in his brain told him that it was just a dream. After all, those particular kinds of monsters didn't *like* his taste. Still, some part of him knew there'd be repercussions someday, even if he tried to live in denial. You don't kill everyone in a town, even a small town like Belasco, without calling at least *some* attention to yourself.

Maybe that's what was happening now?

A sort of monster's revenge?

"Let's go, McSexy," said Granny slapping Azriel's butt and grabbing his hand. She rubbed her thumb up and down Azriel's palm sensuously.

Azriel yanked his hand away.

A chill raced up his spine.

The woman was not only old, but *horny*, too. And she spoke as if she were lusting after him – her supposed grandson.

What kind of deranged family do I have...? he thought, as he followed her to the street.

- 2 -

"All right, hold up," said Azriel. "Tell me what's happened here! Where did those vampires come from?"

"Gawd you're HAWT..." Granny replied, licking her lips and looking Azriel in the eyes like a smitten bride. "If I wasn't your grandma, would you *fuck* me?"

"What the hell's the matter with you," said Azriel. He was already an impatient guy. And this perverted old woman wasn't helping.

"Don't be such a cold fish," said Granny. "Half our family is *inbred*. I still have an egg or two left in me I reckon... and you obviously can't keep a girl *alive*, much less in your bed. Just sayin'."

Azriel felt sick at just the thought of this hag wanting to have sex with him. She was not only disgusting... she was downright crazy.

"Grandma, huh?"

"Yeppers. Can you guess which side? I betchya can't. But no time for a family reunion now, Q-T. We got bigger fishes to bake. We have to go to Belasco. We have to clean up your *mess*."

- 3 -

"What do you mean my 'mess'. I killed all of the zombies. Rawger... the original zombie head... Finius... all of them are locked in uncrackable safes at the bottom of that quicksand pit."

"You really are living, wheezing proof that hot guys are also the dumbest, you know that?" said Granny. "You think I'm talking about *them*? And don't think that Finius stud will stay buried there forever. He's the *slipperiest* man I've ever met. And I ain't just talking about in *bed*, neither."

"You and Finius...?"

"Skinny guy, big, long cock. And a kinky boy to boot, let me tell ya! He liked it rough! He even had a *bleeding* fetish. Can you believe that? Kinkiest sex I ever had!"

Granny licked her pursed lips and her pupils dilated.

After seeing the horrors in Belasco, Azriel thought he was all but numb to being creeped out. But this old hag proved him wrong.

She continued: "You released something that should have stayed buried. Something evil. Something powerful. Something that wants you and me and all the rest of us dead, Dead, DEAD!" Granny slammed her sun-spotted hand into a wall as she said "DEAD!" leaving a crack in it.

Maybe we really are *related*, thought Azriel.

They certainly shared the same temper.

"It almost killed me and it won't stop until it's done the job. These vampires that attacked you are just a small *taste* of what's to come for you. Pawns. They are weak compared to what's waiting in Belasco."

"So tell me who to kill, and I'll do it," said Azriel.

"You couldn't even kill these weaker vampires. The one I'm talking about will tear your dick off and make you *eat* it. Have patience, Boy Toy. We need to get out of the city *pronto*. We don't have a lot of time."

"So what's next?"

"I steal us a car and we scram. Maybe squeeze in a poke at an hourly rate motel on the way. What say you? Hmn?"

Azriel glared at her.

"How'd I spawn such a prude!"

Granny looked back at the burning dumpster as they crossed the street. The flames were dying down. Vampire bodies burned fast. She then looked at Azriel, then back at the garbage, her hand on her bony chin as if deep in thought.

31

"Actually, we're going to make a little detour first."

"Where."

"I hope you like parties," Granny said with her signature cackle.

- 4 -

Granny yanked the car door off a parked 1979 Cutlass and hotwired it.

Azriel kept wondering who *was* this lady? Was she really his grandma?

She was super strong.

Super fast.

Super cunning.

Super old.

And, apparently, super *horny* too. She put her blood-soaked hand on Azriel's knee while driving them through the back streets towards an industrial park. Azriel kept moving her hand away, only for her to put it back and grip his knee again.

"Hand off or I cut it off, get it?" said Azriel.

"Oh goodie! More *rough* sex! Do you promise? Will you make me *bleed* too?"

"You are one sick ass bitch, you know that?"

"Watch that pretty mouth of yours... if I wanted to *rape* you right now I could. And I *would*. You wouldn't be the first. But we're in a hurry. No time even for a *quickie*, I'm afraid."

Azriel wondered if she was serious or sarcastic.

Either way, the thought repulsed him.

"You ready to party, Sexpot?" asked Granny as she pulled the car into what looked like an abandoned warehouse.

The Fenris Tower was clear in the distance again. There was something about that tower that piqued Azriel's interest. He didn't know what it was, exactly. But he had wanted to check it out for months.

"What are we doing here?" asked Azriel.

"Before we go to Belasco, I want to see what you're made of. Those vampires almost killed you without breaking a sweat. You've gone soft. You're a *disgrace*. The way you fought I don't know if you have a dick under that fat belly, or a pussy. I can't bring you with me without knowing you can hold your own. Can't have you getting *me* killed."

"So go without me then."

"You don't understand. You're in this fight whether you want to be or not. *He* is on to you. Knows where you are. He will find you. And he will kill you. That's why we gotta' stick together, Lover Boy. There aren't many of us left and they are gunning for all of us. But I can't have you getting me killed. I need to know you can hold your own — show me you got a ball sack under all that fat."

"So what are we gonna do, arm wrestle to prove myself?"
Granny cackled.

"Oh that's *funny!* I have something a lot more fun in store for you. If you're as powerful as you're supposed to be… I will *love* watching this!"

Granny parked the car and they got out and walked towards the warehouse door. There was a large figure standing in front of it. Loud classical music came from inside. It sounded like Mozart. When they were about 50 yards from the door, Azriel noticed the man standing in front was much bigger than any normal human being. He also wore a tuxedo and had a funny haircut that reminded him of the comic book character "Wolverine."

Azriel figured it must be some kind of party.

Granny wasn't lying about that, at least.

He felt that hot flash of anger and rage swelling up in his belly the closer they got to the thing standing by the door. It was the same rage he was feeling while walking with Mina just before the vampires attacked. The same rage he felt when he was around the zombies. The same rage he felt just looking at a picture of the vampire Anghel "Fezziwig" Belasco and the other monsters in Pastor Shane's monster picture book.

"You know monsters can sense what we are, right? And we can sense what they are, like dogs smelling a cat," said Granny, more a statement than a question.

"Yeah, I figured that out."

Granny cackled again as they got within 20 yards of the door. The hulking figure standing outside it guarding the entrance crossed its arms. "Well then, go sic 'em, little doggy! SIC 'EM!" said Granny as she effortlessly picked Azriel up from behind and threw him – head first – at the guard.

Azriel landed about 5-feet from the door, doing a perfect somersault landing. He looked up at the large figure in front of him. No way is that thing *human*, he realized. It was at least 8-feet tall, and had a thick frame. Azriel guessed it must have weighed 500 lbs.

The swelling pit of rage in his stomach hit him even harder now.

Whatever this thing was, it wasn't human.

It was a *monster.*

And it knew what Azriel was immediately, too.

Both hated each other instantly.

Both wanted to kill each other instantly.

And, both attacked each other instantly.

- 5 -

The creature had a long tongue, cat-like eyes, and fur on its face, head, and hands. It was like a werewolf. Except, instead of being a wolf, it had feline features (*a tiger*, Azriel realized) including a tail – which instantly wrapped around Azriel's neck with a vice-like grip.

It looked at the sky and roared.

Azriel grabbed the tail around his neck and cocked an eye back at Granny.

What did that old bitch just do?

Azriel saw her – a dozen yards away – sitting with her legs crossed. "Don't look at me. You're on your *own* now," she cackled.

Azriel's potbelly heaved up and down as he gasped for breath. He already felt winded. His heart beat so fast he thought he almost might be having a heart attack.

Balls... I'm out of shape, he thought.

But there was no time to worry about that.

The tail choked any air from coming in. The were-tiger hissed, then made a low growl and started to pummel Azriel's face with his large fists, while still choking him with his tail. Granny cackled and cheered as if she were watching a football game. Azriel realized she wasn't joking when she said she wanted to see what he was capable of.

She was watching him.

Testing him.

She wasn't going to save him, he'd have to save himself this time.

And if he didn't do something fast – he'd be dead in mere seconds.

- 6 -

The were-tiger lifted Azriel up with its tail over its head and then slammed Azriel to the ground. Azriel's skull bounced off the pavement like a coconut, and started bleeding. As he hit the pavement, the noose-like tail loosened just enough so Azriel could suck in a short breath, buying him back a little time. It had Azriel pinned to the ground, mouth wide open, teeth bared, roaring in his face, drool dripping onto his forehead.

On pure instinct, Azriel made a fist and shoved it down the monster's throat as far and hard as he could.

The entire length of Azriel's arm went inside.

His fist knocked out three razor sharp teeth on its way down the were-tiger's throat.

Azriel liked the cuts on his fist the teeth made.

In some weird way, Azriel *enjoyed* pain.

It gave him strength and focus.

It made him even angrier.

The tail wrapped around Azriel's neck loosened completely, and the were-tiger's two clawed hands went from punching Azriel to trying to yank his arm out of its throat.

But Azriel wouldn't budge.

He kept stretching his arm farther down its throat, ignoring the pain of its fangs sinking into his skinny arm and bone.

Azriel took a deep breath to get some air and regain his senses.

"You hungry? Want some *num-nums*, you son of a bitch," snarled Azriel grinning and reaching farther down the were-tiger's throat.

Azriel was more than just angry now.

He was *furious*.

This went beyond wanting to escape or survive.

He hated this thing and wanted nothing but to kill it. He couldn't leave without killing it. That Predator instinct was kicking in, making him stronger, impervious to pain, blinded by rage.

Azriel decided he was not just going to kill it.

He was going to make it *suffer*.

Azriel was addicted to this feeling and loved giving in to it. It gave him power – overriding the over-bloated midsection and love handles that were straining his heart and blood vessels, making it hard to breathe, and causing exhaustion far sooner than it normally would. He grabbed the were-tiger's neck and squeezed its throat with his left hand. He inched his right arm even further down the thing's throat, reaching until his arm was shoulder deep inside its mouth. He found something to grab onto, he couldn't tell what, then... yanked as hard as he could. As Azriel pulled it out, the were-tiger slumped over – its left lung in Azriel's bony hand.

It was either dead or passed out.

Azriel figured it was probably just passed out. He had a hard time believing it'd be that easily killed. In the legends, it took a silver bullet to the heart to kill werewolves and, presumably, other were-monsters.

Friggin' disgusting, Azriel thought, as he kicked the were-tiger off him, and tossed the lung towards Granny. The lung hit the pavement in front of her.

Azriel wiped its blood and vomit on its own tuxedo.

His eyes glowed fiery red in the dark.

Granny stood up and looked at the giant lung at her feet.

"Good boy! Yes! Yes! Gooooood boy!" she said clapping her boney hands together. "Now go inside. There are more. They are evil. They are hungry. They are even more *perverted* than your ever-lovin' Granny! Watch your ass!" she cackled.

Azriel stood at the door, panting, regaining his composure.

He didn't need Granny to tell him what was inside.

He could *sense* it.

He knew pure evil lurked within. He knew it was his job to wipe them out. And he knew he would kill everything inside or die trying. It was in his blood and he had no choice. The anger, the rage, the natural instinct to kill monsters took over like a fever. He didn't know exactly what he'd see inside. He still had limited experience with monsters – just zombies, vampires and, now this were-tiger thing.

All he could think about was what else was in there?

What else could he kill?

What other opportunities for a delightful monster *bloodbath* awaited him?

He was no longer scared.

No longer worried.

No longer that fat, flabby, beer-bellied 19-year old who had almost been killed by vampires a couple hours earlier.

He was a Predator.

And, he was *thirsty* for prey.

If his fat belly got in his way, he'd cut it off himself.

Azriel rolled up his sleeves, cracked his knuckles, and kicked the door in.

"Daddy's home, bitches!" he yelled.

The door was several feet away, kicked right off the hinges. As soon as Azriel spoke, the classical music stopped and everyone (every *thing*) in the warehouse went still and stared at him.

Azriel scanned the room.

He'd seen horror when fighting the zombies.

But this was almost as bad – if not worse.

There were cages hung from rafters with dead people – including children – and skeletons inside. Most were half eaten – their guts hanging out, decapitated, with chewed up brains and innards strewn about their cages.

There was a huge bar against the opposite wall.

There were dinner tables with human heads on plates, along with hearts and organs.

The warehouse occupants were all were-monsters.

Azriel counted ten... *things*... total.

One of them was another were-tiger like the door guard Azriel killed. There was also a were-lion. A were-boar. A were-horse. A were-bull. A were-bird that looked like a tall, walking eagle with hands that were talons. There was even a were-lizard and a were-snake – which had two arms, but a snake's body, with a sinister smile darting its tongue in and out. Some of them were sitting at the tables. Some sat at the bar. Some were feasting on human flesh, their mouths still half full when the short kid with the skinny arms and fat belly burst inside. But the two monsters that stood out most were the two *werewolves* – one tall, the other short, almost like a little *brother*, sitting at a private table with two young girls sitting next to them. The children were dirty, scared, and dressed only in shredded panties and torn shirts. They were the only two humans alive in the place. The bigger werewolf was dressed in a tuxedo. Its long mane was slicked back in a ponytail, sunglasses on its face. It had an air of leadership about it. It was in charge – it was the *alpha* in the room. Azriel immediately knew it, just as he knew who the alpha dog was that attacked him and his friends in the Belasco Woods Massacre when he was 11-years old.

He goes down first, Azriel thought.

Within seconds the growling started.

The were-monsters were not happy at having their private party interrupted. And they instantly hated this Predator. They wanted to rend his bones and skin and flesh. They wanted him to die slowly, painfully, and in agony.

Azriel could relate to that feeling.

He wanted to do the same to them.

"You are sick, rabid animals," he said, looking at the cages with the dead and half-eaten children inside, and the grizzly meals served up on trays and platters. "You need to be put *down.*"

- 7 -

Azriel's blood lust took over.

Later, if someone had asked Azriel to recount what happened, he wouldn't have been able to remember much. He didn't have time to think about or process the action. He simply wanted to fight, kill, and destroy. Seconds before the blood lust and violence and carnage began, before he broke bones, shattered jaws, smashed teeth, punched his fists through chests (a neat trick he had to give Granny credit for) and snatching their hearts out... he took a good look at the dead children in the cages, and the human heads on the plates and platters. One even had an *apple* in its mouth. Body parts adorned dinner plates like buffalo wings and chicken dumplings. There were bowls of red oozing liquid – as if they dipped their grizzly meals in blood as sauce. All of this fueled Azriel's desire to kill every last fucking thing inside the building.

He tore through the monsters in his way – as he ran towards the alpha werewolf – like a whirlwind of hate, and violence, and hot, seething anger.

He forgot all about his fat belly.

Forgot about the fact he was working his body so hard, moving so fast, punching so rapidly, that he was vomiting and hacking.

Forgot that he had any limitations – physical or mental – at all.

All he could think of was punishing and killing these monsters which kept blocking his way towards the head werewolf with the fancy tuxedo and sunglasses, and the shorter, "mini-me" werewolf sitting next to him – a dirty, starved little girl on its lap, half conscious and not even aware of what was going on. When Azriel made it to the taller werewolf, Mini-Me werewolf tried to block his way. Azriel dropkicked the midget werewolf's face – knocking it clear across the room, where it smashed into the bar. Azriel then attacked the taller, alpha werewolf, and tried to kill it without mercy or prejudice.

It scratched and punched and kicked Azriel.

It clawed at Azriel's body.

It bit him in the arms and legs.

It even managed to tag Azriel with a series of jabs and uppercuts.

But it seemingly did no good – the unassuming, out-of-shape kid, kept getting up and attacking, wildly, blood-drunk, wanting to kill it.

Azriel bled out of his mouth and his ears.

He could barely *see* out of his swollen eyes.

As the werewolf roared and dug its long claws into Azriel's fat belly, the young Predator grabbed its neck with one hand and with the other plucked its left eye out, and then its right.

The alpha werewolf howled in pain and reeled back.

Azriel's guts felt like they were on fire, but the claw marks weren't deep.

Azriel would live.

And if not, who cares?

At least he would die doing what he *loved*.

The werewolf dropped to a knee and Azriel rammed his entire arm down its throat, just like he did to the were-tiger outside, grabbed its lung and yanked it out. Then, he reached back in and grabbed the other lung. Then he plunged his skinny hands into its chest cavity and pulled out its beating heart, and started tearing it to pieces with his bare hands, turning it into organ meat confetti.

The werewolf slumped to the floor.

But what did the legends say?

What did the TV shows teach?

Werewolves could only be killed with a silver bullet in the heart?

What about just destroying the damn heart?

Azriel tossed the chunks of the alpha wolf's heart into the grill by the bar, which was still burning hot. The flame expanded then shrunk again, as it consumed the heart. The rest of the were-creatures – now trapped – shrunk back, shaking.

Azriel felt the room go cold and still.

Nothing dared make a move.

Nothing dared even breathe loud enough to be heard.

Mini-Me werewolf jumped back onto its feet, growling. He then howled and ran towards Azriel, but jumped completely over him to the taller werewolf's corpse. It cried and looked at Azriel.

"You killed him!" it growled. "You killed my *brother*... we will feast on your heart and your woman's heart and your children's hearts!" it said as it ran out the door.

Azriel let him go.

Mini-Me werewolf was irrelevant, although his gut feeling was to chase him down and kill him. Azriel had a thought that by letting the little shit live, it could cost him dearly later.

He ignored the thought.

Instead, he stayed put and looked around the room, drinking in the fear.

No, it wasn't just fear.

It was *respect*.

Respect from defeating their leader.

Azriel loved the surge of power his anger gave him. He was looking forward to killing as many of these things as possible. It was clear to him, even in his bloodlust state, these were-monsters hadn't seen a predator of his ferocity, or even *heard* of one.

Like all pack animals, they submitted when Azriel killed the leader.

A few of them even started climbing out windows to escape.

No way could Azriel run and catch them all.

Not in his current shape, at least.

But he couldn't just leave like that, either.

He needed to *warn* them.

Needed to leave them with a message.

"Go ahead!" said Azriel out the window they climbed through. He heard one of them mention going back to tell someone named "Fenris" about what happened.

"Yeah, you tell Fenris whoever the fuck he is that this is MY city now. The only reason you are alive is because I *allowed* it!"

Azriel turned back around towards the room.

The two young girls were still alive, sitting on the ground with their knees pulled up to their chests, holding each other's hands, paralyzed with fear.

Azriel scanned the room.

The place was a massacre.

There were still several were-monsters who hadn't left, lying on the ground – either dead or maimed.

Azriel walked over to the girls. "Don't worry. The cops will be here shortly, they'll take you some place safe," he said. He reached into the coat pocket of the werewolf he killed and felt around. Yes, it did have a cell phone. Azriel dialed 911 and told them where he was and to expect a blood bath and he hung up. The cops would have to deal with this on their own.

He sensed something still wasn't right.

He killed the alpha and half the room, but he injured all the rest. The ones left who hadn't escaped out the window were the were-eagle, the were-boar, the were-lizard, and the were-tiger. Their bodies were broken and so in pain they could barely move.

"You're lucky I went so *easy* on you," said Azriel wrapping his arms around the dead alpha werewolf's head. "And that I don't have time to kill you, too!"

Azriel ripped the alpha werewolf's head off.

Blood gathered at his feet from the thing's hairy neck stump.

Two of the were-monsters started urinating their pants, trying to stand.

Azriel ignored them.

He decided to let them go.

He was so tired he could barely stand. But he refused to show it. This was pure animal psychology. He could show no weakness. But he would show mercy. Not because he wanted to; because he could already hear police car sirens and needed to go.

He walked to the door.

His arms and legs quivered from exertion. He was gasping for breath.

His wounds would be okay. His cuts and bruised bones were already healing themselves – a byproduct of his supernatural linage.

Granny waited for him in the doorway. She nodded at him with approval and pride as if she was thinking, *"that's my boy..."*

Azriel scanned the room one more time.

It looked like a tornado hit it.

Tables were flipped over.

Food and flesh and blood covered the floor.

Fur and hair and were-monster body parts and organs littered the ground.

He turned back towards the remaining were-monsters, who were making their way to the window to escape before the police arrived.

"Listen up, listen good, and *never* forget what I'm about to say," said Azriel. "I let you live which means your miserable shitty lives belong to me. If I even so much as hear about any of you sick bastards hurting, killing or even *touching* anyone – especially children – I'm going to hunt down every last one of you sons of bitches, and peel the flesh and fur and scales off your sickly filthy bones. Do you hear me? Do YOU?"

Azriel looked at his blood-soaked hands.

The blood was various shades of orange and swirled together. He smeared some of the blood on his face and clothes, and reached down for the decapitated head he ripped off the head werewolf. This all seemed so familiar to him... so *nostalgic*. He realized he was reliving the Belasco Woods Massacre. And like he did on that day, he put the alpha's head on the top of a broken pool cue on the ground, lifted it up as high as he could, and then tossed it against the wall.

The head hit the wall with a wet thud.

The were-monsters stared at it, horrified.

Azriel walked out the door without turning to look at them.

Granny slapped him on his ass as he walked by.

Azriel turned, panting, his veins sticking out on his neck, forehead, and brow... he was so exhausted he looked like he'd tip over. He looked in Granny's lidless eyes and back handed her so hard, she flew against the car and shattered the driver's side window. One of her last remaining teeth flew out of her mouth.

"Don't ever touch me again you perverted bitch," he said.

4
PLANES, PAINS, AND BAT-MOBILES

"Fly those friendly skies."

- Carl Taylor
Men at Work

- 1 -

Few things ever went right for Fezziwig.

He'd spent many a night lecturing his concubines over the centuries about his bad luck. It seemed like dozens of little annoyances, inconveniences, and aggravations plagued him each day. Some were little things and some were big. Like, for example, he often found himself sitting on the toilet with diarrhea from drinking the wrong blood type, only to realize he is out of toilet paper in the house – with Starr away on an errand, nowhere to be found.

Or ordering a cheese pizza and the idiot pizza place puts garlic on it, which is like *poison* to vampires – swelling up his throat and giving him an asthma attack.

Or when he was in San Francisco and got aroused by a woman he saw, wanted to make her his concubine, brought her all the way home to Alaska, only to find out "she" had a penis.

Or when he was hunting vampires in Asia during his Vampire Purge, and his eyes started failing him due to an allergic reaction. He had to squint his eyes constantly to see signs and people, and the locals started yelling at him, thinking he was *mocking* Asians' eyes.

Or the time he was in New York and thought it would be amusing to wave a dollar in front of a beggar's face and make fun of him, only for the beggar to stick a pencil in his scrotum.

Or the time he took his concubine to the movies, and the guy behind him was making perverted, heavy breathing noises. Fezziwig, without even turning around, threatened to stake the guy through the heart. When the movie finished, Fezziwig saw the poor guy in a wheelchair – with a breathing tube sticking out of his neck, which is what made the noises.

Or the time Starr asked him to take Viagra so he could pleasure her... and his erection lasted 4 months, but he still couldn't ejaculate. And for weeks he kept accidentally putting holes in the dry wall around the house with his rock hard cock.

43

And on and on it went.

Such was Fezziwig's bad luck.

It followed him like a plague. And he never knew what was going to happen next. It was yet another reason he wanted to kill himself. And, it was also why he was so annoyed at the LORD for not letting him.

But the LORD said he had one last task for him.

Except, now there was another piece of bad luck holding him back from doing that: Starr left him the day he was supposed to depart, shortly after his prostate massage.

But she did not leave on an errand.

She left to join what Fezziwig called "the choir invisible."

What happened was that Fezziwig was asleep, resting before leaving for the airport. The Miami Vice theme song was playing at full blast from his old boom box which he kept on a constant loop 24 hours a day, 7 days per week. Starr came in and saw Fezziwig smiling in his sleep and moving his lips, thinking he was talking to her, when really he was just mumbling in his sleep. When she turned down the volume to ask her Master what he was saying, he instantly woke up (he hated anyone touching his Miami Vice music – especially the *volume* – and was even paranoid about it). And with his eyes still crusted shut from his recurring pink eye infection, he blindly grabbed Starr's throat, said "Don't touch my music! Don't touch my music! I don't want to *die* like that!", and tossed her across the room, breaking her neck and killing her.

It was an accident, of course.

He was just too damn paranoid and thought she was something else.

He also felt terrible about it. And foolish. After all, good concubines whom he didn't have to re-educate were near impossible to find since feminism reared its angry head.

Now what was he going to do?

He needed Starr to help him get ready and drive him to the airport. Fezziwig hated driving because driving meant having to get gas. Years ago he was putting gas in the car. And when he got out, he didn't realize he had built up a bunch of static electricity from scuffing his feet on the floor mat. The gas nozzle sparked when he touched it, causing a fire that almost blew him up in his car.

Just more of the infamous Fezziwig bad luck.

With Starr dead, he was finding even trimming his facial hair so it looked like Don Johnson's *Miami Vice* scruff to be a hassle. He couldn't see himself in the mirror (*one of the worst things about being a vampire*, he'd tell his concubines, *is you really don't know what you look like...*), so he didn't know if he had trimmed his facial hair properly. Usually when Starr was away, he took Polaroid pictures of himself to see how he looked when doing his grooming. Whatever made it so he couldn't see himself in the mirror, didn't apply to *film* images. He refused to learn how to use a smart phone or camcorder, and would not adopt modern technology at all. So he would sit while shaving and trimming his facial hairs, taking Polaroid selfies every few minutes to make sure he didn't miss any spots or get anything crooked.

Unfortunately, that damn bad luck hit yet again:

He lost his Polaroid camera.

This was both a good and bad thing, though.

As the only plus to him not being able to see himself in a mirror is not having to look at the sagging "man boobs" he had gained over the years from having lower testosterone and too much estrogen from the blood he drank.

He knew you are what you drink.

And it's not like he could only drink the blood of healthy men with high testosterone levels anymore as he did in the ancient days. Often, he drank blood infested with too much estrogen and other hormones in the water supply that were giving him man boobs, a soft belly, and other feminine features.

But all of these annoyances were the least of his concerns that night.

What was he going to do without Starr's help?

He didn't care so much that she had died. That was par for the course. Most of his concubines ended up killing themselves. Usually they did so after discovering they had just wasted their prime fertile years with Fezziwig, cleaning up his shit, massaging his prostate, and being his servant, and then realizing he never had any intention of turning them into a vampire – never any intention of *promoting* them to immortality – as he'd promised them. When he had no use for them he always sent them away (usually after their 30 birthday, when he would see the noticeable signs of aging). And each time they would ask how he could be so cruel. How could he be so cold? And each time he told them: *"It's nothing that wouldn't have happened to you had you worked in corporate America instead of for me. They also would have taken the best of your talents and your prime fertile years, and then dumped you, too. At least with me, you got to watch some great TV. Now silence yourself and turn* **Miami Vice** *back up!"*

Such was the fate of Fezziwig's concubines.

It mildly amused him before. (Even if he suspected the LORD would not have approved).

But, now that he was without a concubine, and without another waiting in the wings being "trained up" by Starr (with the lie that he needed her to train up a new concubine before turning her into a vampire), he was shit out of luck.

He'd have to drive himself to the airport.

He'd have to get himself ready and packed.

And he'd have to make sure he had all his dozens of meds.

Old Fezziwig always knew life sucked.

And Starr's death (*she knew better than to touch my Miami Vice music!*) was just one more validation of that reality.

- 2 -

Fezziwig managed to do all his packing and was ready to go. But he couldn't shake the feeling he was forgetting something.

What could it be?

He had his meds for his heart, his diabetes, his prostate (*I don't know why I bother taking this shit, it never works*), his hyper tension, his arthritis, his gout, his low thyroid, his high cholesterol, his glaucoma, his low testosterone levels, his high estrogen levels, his pinkeye, his asthma, his allergies (*not that these pills ever do me a damn lick of good...*), his eczema, his dermatitis, his incontinence, his gingivitis, his insomnia, his depression, his recurring urinary tract infection, his various venereal diseases (*I knew I shouldn't have drank all that faggot blood in San Francisco!*)... as well as the meds for his anxiety, forgetfulness, and fatigue. Plus there were all the *other* pills that counteracted the symptoms brought on by his medications.

Fezziwig was truly a miserable wretch.

Many times, with all the diseases he'd gotten from bad blood and meds not interacting right, he'd tell his concubines how he's just one disease away from being a walking *biohazard*. And to make matters worse, Dr. Schumacher refused to see him anymore after he once gave Fezziwig a prostate exam. Fezziwig called the doctor a homo during the exam, backhanded him so hard he flew across the room, and said to never touch him like *that* again.

Fezziwig didn't mean to hurt the guy.

He just didn't like guys touching his asshole.

Only his concubines were entrusted with that noble deed.

And so he found himself on the night he had to leave without a concubine, wondering what he was forgetting. He walked around his small cottage, Starr's corpse's eyes wide open in the corner staring at him, and realized what he was forgetting:

His Bible.

How could he have almost forgotten!

He loved reading his Bible.

He knew every word of it was true, as he had witnessed most of the events inside. The parts he was most concerned with were Ezekiel chapter 31and Revelation chapter 9.

The LORD told him to memorize those passages.

It was essential reading for his mission.

When the LORD told him his orders, he listened. The consequence for disobedience, for not listening to what the LORD told him to do, were too grave, which Fezziwig had learned the hard way 300 years earlier.

And with that thought, Fezziwig picked up his Bible which was from 1611 ("The first King James edition!" he would brag to anyone who listened), read Ezekiel chapter 31 and Revelation chapter 9 one more time, grabbed his two suit cases – one stuffed with clothes, the other with all his pills – piled into his '85 Yugo, and left.

He dreaded leaving his comfortable home.

But, he was happy about one thing.

And that is, he didn't leave very often. But when he did, he made sure he had his Sonny Crockett *Miami Vice* clothes on – including the white sports jacket and pants, the sun glasses, and, of course, the scruffy facial hair.

Old Fezziwig, you sexy son of a bitch, at least you look good!

Or, so he thought.

There was no Starr or Polaroid film to tell him his scruff trim job left uneven patches that looked ridiculous.

- 3 -

Fezziwig almost thought his bad luck had changed when he was early for the first time in his entire 5,500 year life.

He thought for sure his car would have given him trouble. It always did when it was so cold out. But it hung in there like a champ and he got to the airport a full two hours before his flight.

Fezziwig, maybe your luck is finally changing! He thought, as he parked the Yugo. It backfired so loudly, it sounded like a gunshot when he turned the engine off. (*"I told you not to put the cheap gas in there, Concubine! Only the premium gas will keep the car from backfiring when you turn it off!"* he often snapped at Starr). He took his two 1950's era wooden suitcases out of the back, and made his way to the concourse. Fezziwig finally felt optimistic. His luck was always so bad he just came to assume things would go wrong.

But this time, he was early.

When was the last time that ever happened?

Usually he held things up with his bad prostate that seemed never to let him piss. Starr would impatiently tap her foot while waiting. Or the car's bald tired would blow out. Or the battery would die. Or any number of things. Fezziwig didn't like the idea of wasting money on a new car. And, the way he saw it, Starr did all the driving and errand-running for him, so what did he care if it broke down? Let the concubine deal with the car problems. But this time he knew luck was on his side. He was finally early. There was no sudden urge to piss from his prostate forcing him to stop in the middle of nowhere and try to squeeze a few drops out.

There were also no car problems.

No weather issues slowing him down.

No cops trying to pull him over for having no taillights or headlights. (*What do I need headlights for? I see just fine in the dark, Officer...*)

No nothing like that.

Yep, life was good.

He was feeling great, he was on time, and he was going to make that plane without a hitch!

Or so he thought.

When he got to the desk to check his bags he discovered he was late.

Fezziwig misread the ticket through his crusted pinkeye lids.

He thought it said 9:00 p.m., but it had said 6:00 p.m.

At first he yelled at the lady working the counter who thought he was some kind of six-fingered douche bag wearing sunglasses indoors at night. But he looked at the ticket, holding it as far away as possible so his far-sighted eyes could focus, and sure as shit she was *right*.

Dammit!

Fezziwig suddenly regretted threatening to stake the bag check lady through the heart, cut off her head, stuff her mouth with garlic, and then burn her body. He didn't mean any harm. It came out as a reflex.

Luckily she took that as a joke.

Or did she?

As he walked up to the security line, he was immediately pulled to the side for closer inspection. The old TSA agent in the uniform groped his legs, arms, and balls. *That bitch*, Fezziwig thought, *she must have told them to do this. Maybe I should stake her through the heart...!*

Fezziwig assumed all men were gay until proven otherwise. And so, when the TSA agent patted him around the balls, he had to suppress every instinct not to grab the agent by his throat and break his neck. He didn't care too much about human laws or prisons. He'd escaped a lot more dangerous people than the TSA (*Try escaping a burning castle surrounded by hundreds of people with torches and pitchforks,* he once told one of his concubines, *and too nervous to be able to concentrate to turn into a bat. Now THAT's pressure!*)

But before Fezziwig left, the LORD told him to behave.

To not call attention to himself.

To be as *unassuming* as possible.

The LORD's mission was too important. Belasco needed Fezziwig again – and needed him there fast. Time was getting short and the mission needed to be accomplished.

So Fezziwig stayed his hand.

He didn't kill the TSA agent or even flash him an angry look.

He simply grinned, not wanting to show his fangs, and thanked the agent for his time. He even offered to pull his pants and underwear down if the agent wanted a *closer* look to make sure he didn't have a pipe bomb shoved up his ass. Then, without any more drama, the ancient vampire was sent through security to his gate where the next flight to Chicago would depart shortly, assuming he could get on standby.

- 4 -

Fezziwig was starting to think he was screwed.

The standby list was long, and he was at the bottom of it. As they called various people's names, and his wasn't one of them, he was convinced he would be at this airport another day – further slowing him down.

One by one, the standby names were called.

And each time, his name was not one of them.

What would he do if he had to stay at this airport another day? The LORD told him he needed to be in Belasco soon. It was mandatory. No excuses and no delays. The LORD would tolerate nothing less than him being there. The LORD's plan must be fulfilled. The Old and New Testament prophecies must go the way the LORD wanted them to. And Fezziwig was crucial to this happening.

"Michael Dandrige," came the voice. "Come to the front desk."

"Sam Haim," came the voice over the speaker again, "come to the front desk."

"Jerry Farrel," came the voice... "come to the front desk."

"Edgar Feldman," came the voice... "come to the front desk."

Panic set in on the old vampire. The LORD had saved him during the great flood. The LORD had taught him how to survive in a world that would be hostile to him. The LORD even warned him what would happen if he turned anyone else into vampires – which Fezziwig stubbornly ignored, causing himself much regret.

What would the LORD do to him if he was late, he wondered?

How would the LORD *punish* him?

He'd seen how the LORD punished enemies. He was there to witness a lot of those punishments. He did not want the LORD punishing *him*.

Finally, a piece of good luck – the loud speaker said:

"Anghel Belasco, come to the front desk."

They gave him a seat. And not a moment too soon, as the plane had almost fully boarded, and the doors about to be closed.

Fezziwig took his seat.

A window seat.

Good.

That way, he could keep the sunlight out on his side if dawn came when he was still in the sky.

But what about the windows in the other seats?

Dammit!

The captain's voice came over the speaker telling them exactly how long it would be to Chicago and the weather conditions. He also said to expect a beautiful sunrise in a few hours.

Dammit!

Dammit!

Dammit!

The plane started, the doors were sealed, and Fezziwig the vampire was stuck in a plane that, in just a couple hours, would be full of deadly sunlight.

On the *bright* side, he thought, he would get to die, finally.

On the dark side, it would be excruciatingly painful, and the LORD would not be happy.

What was he going to do when the sun rose?

Where would he hide?

These thoughts filled his mind as the plane ascended into the dark sky, with the sunrise not far off.

Then it dawned on him there was only one place he could hide from the sunlight. The one place he would probably have to spend most of the flight in anyway from his bad prostate.

- 5 -

Fezziwig waited until the seatbelt sign shut off and the loudspeaker voice said it was okay to get up and move around the cabin. He knew the sun would be poking through soon and he wanted to secure his spot in the bathroom before someone else did. His life depended on it. Being roasted alive by the sun was the worst possible way he could imagine dying. He remembered killing off many a vampire during the Vampire Purge with sunlight. He would tie them up outside and leave them there all night to feel the sun slowly roast them alive from the inside out at dawn.

It was funny when he did that to *other* vampires.

It was not so funny when he thought of it happening to *him*.

He'd seen how the vampire doesn't just die. He is slowly cooked alive — as if the fire has its own *awareness* that it's killing an unholy entity and wants to take its time. Organs and eyeballs and skin melt slowly. And the vampire doesn't fully "die" until it is completely reduced to ashes.

The process takes hours.

Hours of excruciating pain.

Pain that cannot be stopped with drugs, or alcohol, or pills.

The vampire suffers through it.

All of which is why Fezziwig never killed himself using sunlight before. He'd rather live with his multiple health problems and pains and shitty luck than endure that kind of hellish misery.

Fezziwig was the first in line by the bathroom. Some kid was in there farting and shitting so loudly, the entire First Class section of the plane heard it.

Fezziwig saw the embarrassment on their faces.

It amused him.

But, the sound also made him want to throw up the last meal he had at the airport restaurant: A rare steak (*I want it so rare the damn cow* winks *at me!* He told the waitress. It wasn't the same as human blood, and wouldn't sustain him, but it was still tasty). Plus, he had brought a flask of human blood with him in his carry-on bag and was surprised the TSA faggots didn't confiscate it. Maybe they were too taken aback by his offer to let them inspect his asshole? *Thank the LORD for small favors,* he thought.

The child spent almost an hour inside the bathroom and Fezziwig could see light sky out the nearest window in the distance.

Time was getting short.

Soon the sun would be upon him, killing him slowly, *sizzling* his heart, and liver, and lungs, and kidneys, and eyeballs.

What the hell was taking this kid so long? Constipation?

By his estimate, Fezziwig didn't think the sunlight was more than a few minutes off now.

He was getting nervous.

Antsy.

Almost ready to rip the door off, throw the kid out, and then capture the bathroom for his own. But if he did rip the door off he'd be naked to the sunlight again.

Dammit!

Dammit!

Dammit!

DAMMIT!

The light got closer, Fezziwig could feel the heat – like a sunburn – hit his neck, and flipped his collar up. He looked like a cross between Dracula and Sonny Crockett himself.

This is it.

Killed waiting for a bathroom.

Just my bloody luck.

Why am I not surprised...?

The sunbeams came in, and he put his coat over his head. It helped, but the movies got it wrong not realizing that the sun could kill a vampire even through clothing. Especially white clothing like his.

His skin started to blister and smoke and sizzle.

His eyes got dry.

A hot pain ran down his spine and into his bones.

This is it.

The end.

Sorry LORD... I tried, have mercy on me?

As he prepared to accept his fate, the door opened.

The kid inside walked out and giggled.

Fezziwig, with thin wisps of smoke floating off his body, shoved the kid out of the way, ran inside, and locked the door. His hand burned the kid's shirt and left a six-fingered hand mark like an iron had been left too long on it. The child screamed out.

I must have slightly burned him.

Dumb kid, that's what you get for being a little shit.

Fezziwig smiled.

He was still alive and his mission still intact.

Thank the LORD.

- 6 -

There were still three hours left of his flight when Fezziwig barreled into the bathroom. He figured it would take at least that long to piss anyway due to his rotten prostate. He heard a line forming outside the bathroom growing onto the one that was already there waiting for that kid before Fezziwig got inside.

The smell sickened Fezziwig.

What did that little faggot eat?

And to make matters worse, the people outside were groaning and complaining about him taking too long. There were knocks on the door. People were getting anxious. They had to piss and shit and do the things people all wait to do when they get on a plane, instead of doing it beforehand.

The hell with them.

They should have been faster.

Fezziwig's skin started to heal itself from the sunlight and he was feeling a lot better. Even his prostate was letting up a bit as he sat on the toilet, and a few drops squeezed through. Fezziwig was stuck in there until the plane landed. And even then, he'd have to wait until dark to leave the bathroom.

One thing at a time, Fezziwig, he thought.

Right now it's time to relax and focus.

Focus on the mission.

Both missions.

The LORD gave you a job, don't be a pussy.

Fezziwig knew he would have obstacles when he got to Belasco. The LORD told him the vampire *Rood* would stand in his way. Fezziwig thought he had killed Rood. He thought he had done the deed right: Staked the evil son of a bitch through the heart, cut off his head, stuffed his mouth full of garlic, and burned and buried the body in the only place on earth that would *keep* it from coming back.

Except it didn't.

The LORD said Rood was in Belasco.

The LORD said Rood needed to die.

The LORD said a Predator would help Fezziwig do the deed.

Good.

Fezziwig would need the help.

As much as he hated to admit it, he would need help to kill Rood once and for all, and especially to complete his *other* mission the LORD gave him.

And this time, Rood would stay dead.

- 7 -

Fezziwig snapped out of his thoughts when a particularly forceful fist pounded the door and a key was jiggling in trying to open it. Fezziwig held the door, his vampire claws extended, sunk into the plastic, not letting it open. He was ten times stronger than any human was, even at his age and with all this ailments. And as long as he was alive, that door was not going to open. Fezziwig heard the voices outside yelling at him, saying the plane was landing, and he had to take his seat and buckle up. When he stubbornly refused and told them he couldn't get off because he was sick and shitting all over, it seemed to shut them up. They told him to stay seated and hold on as they prepared to land.

For now, the flight attendants were cooperating.

Good.

But, what would he do when they landed? It was broad daylight now. He had to stay in that bathroom until it was dark.

The plane landed and the other passengers left. The flight crew knocked again.

"Sir you have to go, we have to prep this plane to fly out again in an hour."

"Too bad. I can't. I'm shitting bricks in here! Find another plane," said Fezziwig.

He didn't know how much longer he could hold them off before they would force the door open, overpowering even him if they used tools, and let the sunlight in.

"Let me ask you a question," said Fezziwig.

"What?"

"Are we parked in shade, is sunshine coming in through the windows?"

"No, there is sun. Sir, you must go."

"I can't. Is there sunlight hitting the bathroom door?"

"No. Sir, I am not asking again," came the stewardess's voice.

"Okay, I'm coming out. But stand back, it *stinks* in here!"

Fezziwig needed a clear path. Any sunlight in the corridor could kill him.

He unlocked the door and ran out.

Sunlight hit him and his body began to blister and smoke.

The two flight attendants jumped back out of his way. He saw sun coming in from every direction: the pilot's cockpit window, the first class section windows, and even peaking in from the mechanism that connects the plane door to the gate.

"Shit!" he yelled as he looked up.

His body started to catch on fire.

He looked at the ceiling.

It was not being touched with sunlight.

Fezziwig closed his eyes, concentrated, and his clothes fell to the ground. It looked like he vanished. The pilot was watching through the cockpit door and the two attendants looked like they saw a ghost. For that brief moment nobody noticed the bat flying across the ceiling, away from the sunlight, and into the airport.

Fezziwig was without clothes.

He was without his bags.

And, he was without his meds.

He figured he'd have to find a place to hide inside the airport then depart at sunset – flying all the way to Belasco "bat mobile."

Once again Fezziwig thought about how he always knew life sucked.

And, once again, here was one more validation of that reality.

5
THE PRODIGAL RETURNS

"So, you came back to die with your city."

- Bane
The Dark Knight Returns

- 1 -

"Enough tests, no more bullshit. Why are these vampires trying to kill me... us... whatever," said Azriel looking out the car window. He was still out of breath, face red from exhaustion, and wiping off the orange were-monster blood he painted on his face. He felt like he'd just run a marathon. He was too exhausted to even sit up straight.

"They hate you," replied Granny.

"I haven't seen or heard a peep out of anything in a long time. No monsters. No zombies. Nada."

"You've covered your tracks good. But you're sexy-as-hell 'Nana never lost track of you. Never stopped checking in on the baby to make sure he's *safe,*" replied Granny followed by a cackle. "But it's more than that. The entire monster underworld is scared of you after what you did in Belasco. They'll be even *more* scared of you after tonight, eh? What do you think of that, Sir Cunt-A-Lick?"

"Enough with the perverted crap. You didn't have to trick me. I haven't been able to cut loose in so long. I *wanted* it."

"Wrong-o, Bitch Boy. You're powerful. At least you *should* be. But you've gotten complacent. Look at you. You're still breathing heavy. We left there 20 minutes ago! I have to admit though, Baby Doll, you did your ever lovin' grand-mammy *proud.* I thought you were a total pussy. Those vampires would have ripped you to shreds if I hadn't interfered. But them were-monsters will be pissing their pants out of their little pricks at the *thought* of you. But there's one vampire who ain't scared of you. And he wants you dead, dead, DEAD!"

Granny floored the car with that last "dead" and cackled.

Azriel was unfazed.

He was too deep in thought and too exhausted to react.

"Tell me about this vampire. I want to know everything."

"His name is Rood. And he's a powerful sonuvabitch let me tell ya, Sex Toy. And he wants all us Predators dead – especially *you.*"

"He's just a vampire."

55

"Oh he's much more than that. *Much* more."

"Tell me everything."

- 2 -

For the next several hours, as they barreled down Route 57 in the odd hours of the early morning, Granny told Azriel about the vampire who wanted him dead.

The only name she had for him was "Rood."

None of the Predators knew much else about him.

The only known living vampire was Anghel Belasco. But he hadn't been seen in over 100 years. He was completely off the grid if he was still alive at all. In recent months there had been vampire "sightings" in Belasco, Illinois. Most of these sightings were written off as hallucinations. And the strange disappearances of motorists and drifters who passed through over the last six months were ignored or covered up. Granny said the government had long employed Predators as monster "bounty hunters." She also said the government covered up a lot of monster killings and sightings but nobody knew for sure, because every Predator bounty hunter she'd met had gone dark – never heard from again. Police and other reports were written off as pranks, gags, or quicksand deaths. But the last handful of living Predators still left knew something *else* was going on. And some, like Granny, went to investigate. Rumors of a war – an alliance of the various monsters banding together – had been brewing for years. And the Predators all took particular interest in Belasco after Azriel killed all the zombies. They knew there was something evil going on there. And the fact Azriel – or *Azrael*, as most of the other Predators called him – was at the center of the zombie deaths, put the small Illinois town back on the map.

The only thing the Predators Granny talked to knew about Rood was this: He was an especially *strong* and gruesome vampire.

He was also capturing, torturing, and killing Predators, while setting up his base of operations in the Belasco ghost town. Instead of going forth into the world, as the vampires of old did, with no leadership, no direction, and causing chaos and bringing attention to themselves, they were holing up.

One by one, Predators who investigated went missing.

Granny went to check it out as well.

She, too, fought with Rood and his new vampire gang in Belasco three weeks earlier. She was captured, tortured, and partially skinned alive. Rood's concubine (*"a particularly nasty cunt of a vampire!"* she said) even sliced off Granny's eyelids.

Rood *enjoyed* causing pain and tormenting people.

Peoples' screams gave him a sick, *sexual* pleasure. Granny noticed a large hard-on form in Rood's pants when his concubine cut into her when she was on the torture table. He killed his own vampires for the slightest of offenses. Granny witnessed Rood kill one of his own vampire spawns because a drop of blood plopped on his wrist when the vampire lackey poured him a glass.

Rood was stronger than any vampire she'd ever heard of.

She had no idea how he got that powerful.

But he was at least eight-feet tall by her guess.

Granny said she was one of over a dozen predators being tortured simultaneously. She heard Rood say he would prop himself up as master of the world when he won the war he was about to start. But he was eliminating Predators, first. He needed them out of the way.

There was one Predator he was especially keen on killing:

The boy who single-handedly destroyed the zombies.

The vampires were *nervous* about him.

The boy was not to be underestimated.

He was to be brought back – dead or alive, but *unspoiled*.

"At first, I couldn't understand what the big dealy-bop was about you," said Granny. "You're slow. Easily taken. I could snap you in half now if I wanted, you little fatty fucktard. Nobody trained you. Pastor Shane and his idiot friends in The Order kept me away from you for years – hiding you in plain sight in that God-forsaken town. When I found you tonight I almost left you to die after your embarrassing performance. But you redeemed yourself! Oh, yeah, you redeemed yourself! My arid cunt got wet just *watching* you... just *thinking* about it!"

Granny cackled and floored the car again.

"I assume you have a plan," said Azriel. "Unless you're planning on *humping* this Rood thing to death."

The old woman put her hand on Azriel's knee. Azriel grabbed her thin wrist and squeezed as hard as he could. Granny winced in pain.

"I told you..." said Azriel, throwing her arm back into her own lap.

"Sorry, Sexy, can't help it. You're just so fucking HAWT!" Granny smiled through her few remaining teeth and licked her lips. "The plan is simple," she said. "We drive into Belasco and attack in the day when they are sleeping and not expecting *me*. I escaped. They think I'm in hiding. We take the fight to Rood and surprise him. We take him down, and drag him by his cock into the *sunlight*. Together we might have a chance."

Azriel grinned.

This horny old woman disgusted him.

But he liked her plan.

The idea of making this Rood thing, whose henchmen killed his girl right in front of him, die in the sunlight was appealing. He was already coming down off the high of the fight with the were-monsters and could use another "fix" as far as he was concerned. He would go with Granny and play his part in this bizarre chess game of Predators and vampires.

He would fight with her.

And, he would *win*.

Azriel's eyes glowed red as he thought about all the wonderful ways he wanted to punish this Rood vampire. Granny's lidless eyes caught a glimpse of his red eyes. She was turned on by how he dug his fingers so hard into the seat he punctured the leather.

The boy was more powerful than she thought.

- 3 -

"What about our mental abilities. I was able to control the zombie's minds. All that happened when I tried it on the vampires was one of them turned into a *bat*," said Azriel.

The sun was fully up and it was well past 8:00 am.

"That old shit Pastor Shane should never have kept you from the truth. He *castrated* you with those blue pills, didn't he? Yes, some of us have psychic abilities. Our family all do. But it's different for everyone. And it has a different effect on each monster. Mind fucking the way you did it controlling zombie brains is a new one. One of our ancestors had that gift against zombies. Too bad for him he up and croaked before anyone could ask how. Otherwise we can do little things – like make them see something that's not there briefly or make a monster suddenly feel too cold or too hot. Nothing permanent. Nothing that doesn't give us just a *moment's* edge in a fight. You, Sexy Pot, must have abilities none of us have. Mind control... I never seen that. You have more power than I ever saw from a Predator. The way you tore into all those were-monsters at the warehouse... my vajay-jay was all-a-*tingle* after watching that!"

More cackling.

She reached over and tried to put her hand near Azriel's crotch.

Azriel grabbed her hand and tossed it back towards the steering wheel.

"What the hell is *wrong* with you?," asked Azriel.

"Don't be such a prude, Hawt Stuff," she replied, darting her tongue out and then making a smooching sound with her thin, pursed lips.

"Sick bitch. Tell me something. What happens when you use your mental abilities on a vampire?"

"Nothing," she replied.

"I thought we all had this ability."

"I fought those shit-tards almost to the death last time and nothing happened. It's just the way it is. Don't count on that working for you like it did before. Turning them into bats could have its *usefulness*, though. Right now you wield your power like a clumsy retard. I don't know if you'll be enough for us to kill Rood, but we will see, eh?"

They remained silent the rest of the drive.

Yes, they would confront Rood and bring the fight to him.

He'd never expect it.

At least, they *hoped* he wouldn't.

Otherwise, Granny insisted they were both as good as dead.

- 4 -

Azriel and Granny reached the off ramp to Belasco after noon. They had decided earlier to stop at a rest area and try to get a few hours' sleep. They would need it if they wanted to kill Rood.

When they pulled onto the ramp Granny said to be cautious. Some of the old vampire weapons she used didn't work against Rood. She plunged a wooden stake directly into his heart. He simply pulled it out as casually as if he was scratching a mosquito bite. It didn't even *tickle* him.

She said their best bet was sunlight.

They could go into his crypt while he's sleeping and drag him out into the rays. Cook him in his sleep when he's defenseless.

She said speed was necessary. Whatever Rood was planning, was going to happen soon. And the fact he was hunting down predators was especially alarming.

Few monsters did that anymore.

Most of them wanted to *avoid* Predators.

Azriel remembered Pastor Shane teaching him about this.

He told Azriel it was the Predator's job to hunt down and kill monsters. That was what they were bred for all those centuries ago after Noah's flood, when more fallen angels returned to earth again to impregnate the daughters of men and those daughters birthed more monstrosities – *giants.* They were also known as the Nephilim or "Fallen Ones." They were the demigods and monsters talked about in Greek, Sumarian, Norse, Babylonian, and other ancient mythologies. They were inherently evil, unusually wicked, and supernaturally powerful. The angels who sired them completely corrupted mankind's genetic lines until only Noah and his wife, his sons and their wives were still genetically pure. Every man, woman, and child was either a hybrid, killed by the hybrids, or, in the case of women, marrying the fallen angels and siring more hybrid children. Had God not sent the flood, they would have taken over everything, and polluted the seed line of the Messiah – Jesus Christ.

The post-flood people decided to fight back in their own way, despite God not telling them to. They bred their own kind of genetic hybrids using knowledge the fallen angels taught them in exchange for their women. They called their hybrids Predators. Strong, violent, hard to kill – these Predators were "programmed" to hunt down and kill Nephilim without God's consent. God told the Israelites to do that job. It was their God-given duty to wipe them out. A few Israelites did, including a young David who bested one with a pebble. But most of the Israelites ignored their duties and let many Nephilim get away. The Nephilim immediately went into hiding.

The Predators continued hunting them down and killing the leftover Nephilim and their children through the centuries. But eventually, many of the Predators started to abuse their power. They set themselves up as dictators and gods, keeping humanity down and under their oppression – an even worse oppression than the Nephilim created. Pastor Shane explained that Predators like Azriel were *abominations* to God. They were not part of His plan. They were as profane and unclean as the monsters they were bred to kill. Pastor Shane told him this the night he died, when the Pastor's own kin Finius – who somehow hybridized himself with zombies, taking on certain of their attributes – betrayed him.

Azriel took care of Finius, though.

He let Finius find him in Chicago, seized control of his mind, fed him to the original zombie head, and put his remains in two safes – his head in one, his bodily remains in another. Then, he cast the safes into the quicksand pit where he has been rotting for the last year.

At least, he assumed Finius was still there.

What was it Granny said about him?

He's *slippery?*

Azriel agreed.

Finius *was* slippery.

Granny stopped the car and pulled over midway down the ramp.

"Why not just crash right into Rood's crypt. Go in hard and fast," said Azriel.

"Hard and fast... I like the way you *think*. I'm going to get you in the sack yet, Sexy," said Granny.

"Disgusting."

Granny winked at Azriel and blew him a kiss. "Look," said Granny pointing to the road with the big stop sign at the end of the ramp. There was a school bus and a sailboat on a trailer blocking the exit. Unless they had a motorcycle, there was no way they were driving in via the main road that went through Belasco anyway. They'd have to foot it. The graveyard where Rood set up his headquarters and tortured Granny was on the other side of town. It'd take them almost an hour to walk there.

Granny exited the car and opened the back door to get her large pack out stuffed with wooden stakes, garlic, lighter fluid, matches, and full water vials.

"Holy water?" asked Azriel holding one of the vials up in the sunlight.

"Yeppers."

"Do you think it will work on Rood?"

"Don't know. Didn't have a chance to use it on him," said Granny – her lidless eyes stared right into Azriel's with a mixture of lust and wonder. It gave Azriel the creeps. "We'll get our chance to try it. For now probably best not to count on it, eh? Now shut your pretty lips up and let's go."

- 5 -

As they walked down Belasco's empty streets the reason revealed itself why Azriel hadn't heard anything about the town in the past year:

Belasco, Illinois had been completely abandoned.

Granny was right when she called it a ghost town.

There was no way to drive into town so people naturally just turned away off the ramp. Drifters, looters, and anyone wanting to come in through the road that went through the center of town, could stop by. But chances are they were ambushed by Rood and his minions. And since the entire population was wiped out, nobody had any explanation how, and the government was covering things up, so superstition did its job.

"I have another question," said Azriel as they walked past a storefront he remembered visiting as a kid. It had a big sign that said *Ash's Music Lessons*. "You mentioned something called 'The Order.' Tell me what you know about them."

"No more questions, Porky," she replied. "Time to focus. You're already fatigued. Look at you."

It was true.

Azriel's large belly and quick fatigue was slowing them down. He was also craving something sweet – and imagining a handful of delicious Hot Tamales candies in his mouth. If nothing else, he thought about how he could sure go for a frosty LandShark beer with a fat lime wedge. And why not? He deserved a beer after wiping out all those were-monsters. But there was no candy or beer for him. Maybe there never would be again. That notion saddened him. He was already breathing hard and they hadn't even walked more than 100 yards, and that was downhill. The were-monster fight had his entire body feeling like it'd been pelted with stones as it rapidly tried to heal itself. But he wasn't going to let this old hag know it by telling her. He could just imagine the perverted bitch saying, *"Want a massage, Sonny Boy? I'll even give you a happy finish!"* with her creepy cackle.

"All right, but one thing I have to know. You said I started this. That it was *my* fault. How?"

"Something to do with the explosion you set off. Maybe you can ask him before he cuts off *your* eyelids, eh?"

She had a point.

If Rood was as powerful as she said he was, Azriel needed to not care about these trivial questions and focus. If this bastard was anything close to as strong and dangerous as Chief Rawger was, it really would take both of them to kill it.

Granny led them down to the intersection of Barnabas and Collins streets, which was odd to Azriel, considering that was the opposite way as the graveyard.

"Thought we were going to the graveyard," said Azriel.

"We're making a pit stop. Pastor Shane had a secret room, no? I never found it. But I know it's there. And I suspect you know about it. Yes?"

"Lots of books, food, water, a panic room." The thought of resting there appealed to Azriel.

"I think we should go there first. See if he had any info on Rood. I want any advantage we can get," said Granny. Her cackle and perverted talk were gone.

Azriel wondered why he didn't think of that himself. He didn't spend much time there that night before Pastor Shane died. But he did remember all the books lying around and in the bookcase. Maybe there would be something there? Pastor Shane had info on Anghel Belasco, so maybe he had something on Rood, too?

Only one way to find out.

As they approached the church Azriel remembered all the Sundays he spent there farting in his pew for attention and abhorring all the talk about holding hands and loving each other. He always preferred the parts of the Bible about people being killed, smitten, and beheaded. Why couldn't church be more about that? Why all the gay hand-holding and singing? It was something he'd thought a lot about as a kid.

The church doorway was exactly as Azriel last remembered it: Chief Rawger had kicked the door off and there was no door. Rawger's squad car was still outside, covered in bird poop. It was weighted down from supporting the zombie's enormous bulk, and the tires were completely flat. The basement door was also just as he remembered it: The stairway completely collapsed from when he fought Rawger. Except, there was something weird about the whole thing. The place looked... *tidy*, almost. As if someone had been down there organizing or looking for something.

All the piled wood was pushed to the sides.

There were footprints in the dust, too.

Strange.

Azriel started to get that pit in his stomach telling him something was wrong. Something evil was afoot. Something he hated and wanted to kill was nearby. But what could it be?

This was Pastor Shane's secret bunker. It was safe.

Must just be nerves, he figured, ignoring the warning.

"Down this way," said Azriel leading Granny to the secret door into

Pastor Shane's panic room. He looked for the small knot he remembered seeing Pastor Shane push. It took a few moments to find it, but there it was. He pushed it. There was the same clicking sound Azriel remembered last time, and the door opened. "It's through here," he said as he walked in. The old woman followed so close he could feel her lightly brushing up against him. Azriel turned and looked at her – ready to tell her to quit being such a perverted old cunt. Her lidless eyes seemed even wider than usual. She looked serious, not horny.

When he entered he realized why:

The room wasn't empty.

There was a tall female with breasts so large they practically fell out of her top. Her figure instantly reminded Azriel of Jessica Rabbit from the *Who Framed Roger Rabbit?* movie. She had a rusty straight razor in her hand. Two men were standing with her. They each had chalk white skin and long fingernails. The room smelled like death.

Jessica Rabbit vampire shot them a fanged smile.

"So good of you to join us Azriel," she said. Her accent was Eastern European, like something out of an old horror movie. "I've heard so *much* about you."

Azriel turned around towards Granny again. She lifted her leg to kick the large oak book case door shut behind them, locking them in.

Granny smiled.

But there was no cackle.

- 6 -

The two male vampires were easy pickings for Azriel.

Before anyone had a chance to attack him, he donkey-kicked Granny in the stomach behind him, knocking her down. Next, he was upon the closest vampire, wrapped his arms around its head, and ripped it clean off. He tossed the fanged faced head – still attached to its spine – at the other male vampire. As that one reflexively caught the head, Azriel dove into it shoulders first and, taking a page right from his treacherous Granny's playbook, plunged his fist as hard as he could into its chest, and pulled out its still-beating heart. He was finding that maneuver endlessly useful.

But that was all the triumph Azriel had.

Jessica Rabbit vampire's hand grabbed his neck. She dug her nails into his flesh, then yanked and slammed him into the secret oak book case door, crashing right through it. Dozens of books and wooden parts piled on top of Granny. The rest were scattered on the ground outside the room were Azriel sat, near the demolished stairway. Granny and the Jessica Rabbit vampire who tossed him were inside – and shocked by the speed and ferocity of the fat young Predator.

The female vampire was told Azriel was powerful. But this was beyond anything she'd seen before.

Vampires, after all, had their own superhuman abilities: speed, endurance, strength. But this kid who barely looked like he shaved, with the big potbelly, wheezing and panting out of breath, had killed two vampires within a matter of seconds.

Azriel took advantage of the situation and darted towards the broken staircase. He jumped up to the next floor, and ran out of the church. He ran so fast he would have been almost a blur to anyone watching. The first thought going through his brain was how he'd just been betrayed by Granny.

That bitch!

That perverted, sick, treacherous bitch!

I knew she was up to something.

Could see it in her bulging freaky eyes.

She'll be the first one I kill…

- 7 -

Azriel's next thought was to flee into the Belasco Woods.

Those evil, dark, menacing woods had saved him twice before. The first time was when Dr. Crowley was looking for him, chasing him, wanting to kill him, as Azriel was crippled by the blue pills, making his every movement, breath, and thought agonizing pain. The second time the woods saved Azriel was when he led the zombie hoard into the thick of the forest. He seized their minds and led them to an old shack full of dynamite and explosives, and destroyed them all.

The woods were evil.

He always knew it even as a child.

But he also *knew* those woods.

Knew them probably better than anyone.

He needed time to make a plan.

Time…

What time was it? They'd gotten to town at some time past noon. Judging by the sun, it was almost 2:00. Where did the time go?

Azriel looked back and stopped for a quick breather. His lungs felt like they were full of fire, he could barely breathe, and was already sweating as if he'd been sitting in a sauna. At least he didn't see Granny following him. The big-breasted vampire wouldn't be able to follow him in the sun, which means he only had to worry about Granny.

He'd have a much easier time killing her alone.

Azriel ran up to the woods and skirted around to the secret trail he and his friends used on the day of the Belasco Woods Massacre.

Yes, he would go to the woods.

He'd go there and hide.

And wait.

And plot his revenge.

That bitch Granny would pay for what she did. And when he was done with her, he'd kill this Rood asshole, too, and the chick vampire with the perfect tits and ass.

But that was later. Now, he needed to catch his breath. He was so exhausted he sat against a tree, and fell asleep thinking:

How the hell did I let myself get this fat and out of shape...

Ben Settle

6
THE LIFE AND DEATH OF RORY ROOD

"You made me. Remember? You dropped me into that vat of chemicals. That wasn't easy to get over, and don't think that I didn't try."

- The Joker
Batman

- 1 -

During the early, pre-dawn hours when Azriel and Granny were driving from Chicago to Belasco, "bat-mobile" Fezziwig flew towards the same location.

As a vampire-turned-bat he flew faster and had more stamina than an ordinary vampire bat. He still possessed his vampire form's strength and power, it was just "compressed" and proportional to his size. He flew high enough to stay out of sight of anyone on the ground. He also listened for incoming predator owls that may want to make him a snack. He couldn't have any delays. He thought about the time he was snatched up and swallowed whole by a hungry owl. To save himself, he turned into his normal humanoid form while going down the owl's throat, scattering the owl's body into dozens of chunks of meat and fur.

It was a nasty business.

And the smell was *horrible.*

It took days to get the smell out of his *nostrils* and pick all the pieces of owl out of his hair, since he couldn't see in the mirror. As his bad luck dictated, he was all out of Polaroid film and his concubine was out of town on a blood run.

There were more pressing things on his mind besides owls and people who might see him.

He was racing against the sunlight again.

He waited all day in O'Hare Airport's air ducts trying to figure out a way he could get his bags and meds. But he couldn't think of anything that would allow him to do it inconspicuously. The LORD was very firm on him not revealing his true self to anyone until he got to Belasco. And, even if he had, he was naked. Getting a car like that in time to speed down route

67

57 before the sun came up would be impossible. Normally he'd have taken vampire form in a gift shop, grabbed one of the lame Chicago tourist sweatshirts and shorts being sold, then make a run for his bags at the baggage claim, and skim through the shadows until he could find a cab.

But no such luck. He had to remain incognito. He couldn't risk being seen, caught, or detained. Not even for a few minutes.

Fezziwig went through a lot of trouble to make sure he killed all the vampires off during the great Vampire Purge. He did it after realizing what an undisciplined chaotic bunch of emotional candy-ass faggots they were. They couldn't control their thirst for blood. Nor could they resist turning beautiful women they bit into vampires — foolishly thinking those women would be obedient and submissive. Fezziwig knew, as his spawns came to know, that female vampires were more unruly, more unpredictable, more seductive, more manipulative, and more emotionally unstable than even human women were. They were violent tempered and needed constant attention, validation, and praise or they turned nasty. Their flurry of feelings caused many of the female vampires to rip out men's throats, seek revenge against guys who *spurned* them in their past when they were still human, and make men their *slaves...* only to find they had lost all attraction for those men after they got everything they wanted, and then killed them anyway.

Oh what a mess his idiot vampire spawns made.

In the Middle Ages, the world knew of Fezziwig and his vampire spawn. Back then it was not uncommon for a vampire to be chased by people out of the country or killed. And Fezziwig, even though he was careful and didn't want any trouble, was always being caught in the crossfire.

When he killed all the vampires, he figured he was done cleaning up their messes.

Until now.

Rood was back.

Somehow returned from the dead — and from a prison he couldn't possibly have escaped.

Rood was the one who inspired Fezziwig to kill all the other vampires in the first place. He was the worst of the lot — the one who made Fezziwig realize what a fool he'd been to not listen to the LORD, who told him *not* to turn anyone else into a vampire thousands of years earlier.

How did Rood survive?

And how did Rood grow as powerful as the LORD described him?

With those questions, as bat-mobile Fezziwig flew through the night sky, he searched his fuzzy memory for the time when it all started. When he found, turned, and then killed the Pastor Rory Rood...

Fezziwig found Pastor Rory Rood in the late 1600's. The Pastor was an Irishman who was against all wars, for any reason, and despised violence.

He was a man of peace.

A man who hated the thought – much less the sight – of bloodshed, especially *innocent* bloodshed.

He pastored a small community church in North Carolina – not far from Roanoke, where an entire colony had gone missing several years earlier. Pastor Rood was strangely attracted to that area. He didn't know why. But he felt an evil presence there. He thought it was his job, as a man of God, not to avoid that evil, but to confront and *defeat* it in the name and blood of Jesus Christ, and with the power of His love. And so he moved his family there, founded a church, and tried to live peacefully. He had a big family, read his Bible a couple days per year (trusting in the Holy Spirit to guide his decisions more than the antiquated book that promoted war and bloodshed in its Old Testament), and had taken a pacifist view of life. He hated violence so much, he refused to eat meat or let his family eat meat. He made his wife and five children eat berries and whatever vegetables they could grow on their small farm. They all ate like rabbits. And all but the wife were weak, skinny, gangly looking as such. Somehow, his wife was grotesquely fat – taking up three seats in the pew. Pastor Rood wondered how his wife got so large. Especially the way they ate.

The irony amused Fezziwig.

Rood was the most peaceful and non-violent man he'd ever heard of. Yet, with one bite to his neck (*in his own church*), Fezziwig thought it'd be amusing to turn such a peace-loving man of the cloth into a vampire. The result was the most vicious, bloodthirsty, and reckless vampire the world had ever seen.

Maybe it was pent-up rage suppressed by Rood's pacifism.

Maybe it was his sky-high estrogen levels from never eating meat and only eating vegetables and soybeans.

Maybe it was a genetic predilection to violence.

Or, maybe the Pastor Rory Rood deep down *liked* the evil inside him. Maybe he was *seduced* by the evil of that part of the New World, and not merely attracted to it as something to combat with love as he thought.

Who knew what it was?

What Fezziwig did know was Rood's sudden change made the ancient vampire realize what a mistake it was turning anyone else into vampires. Fezziwig had created something that was so reckless and thirsty for violence, it would bring attention to their kind in ways that would get him hunted down and destroyed. But this time, it wouldn't be torches and pitchforks attacking Fezziwig. Humans had better and ever-increasingly powerful weapons: Like muskets, gun powder, and cannons – things that could be turned into a Predator's tools of death.

The LORD had told him – after the great flood wiped out his Nephilim brothers and cousins – not to spawn other vampires.

But did Fezziwig listen?

At first, yes.

But as the centuries stretched on, he got bored and lonely.

He wanted beings he could relate to.

He wanted a family to have his back.

But with Rood, he realized any of his children could be a threat to him – either directly, or through bringing attention to their race. He decided to start his Vampire Purge with Rood. There was something about Rood that frightened Fezziwig.

The fallen angel blood Fezziwig passed on to Rood now running in his veins turned him into something far more *sinister* than any of his other ilk.

- 3 -

The first thing Rood did after being bit by Fezziwig was slaughter his family. He'd never dare admit it to himself before that night – but somewhere tucked inside his mind, he secretly despised them. He hated having to feed their hungry mouths. But he was especially repulsed listening to his fat wife (*How did she get so fat anyway? Where was she hoarding the food?*) who was always complaining about not having enough to eat, and calling him a fool and coward for handing over money to thieves and beggars in church without making them work. He constantly stressed over how he was going to pay for them with money that was never enough due to his small church, which catered to "saving" the lazy, the slothful, and the wicked. Rood thought it was his job not to avoid the sick, but to be *amongst* them. To be their healer. To lead them not by scripture, but by his *example*. And so he violated what his own Bible told him, and let all the unrepentant sinners in his church he could: the slothful, the sodomites, the murderers, the thieves, and the defilers of children. He sometimes even hid them from the law when they asked.

It was Rood's job, he believed, to help save these lost.

Not to punish them or rat them out.

That was why he believed he was *led* to be a pastor. But deep down, somewhere, he knew it was wrong. He knew he was being *disobedient*. He really wanted the world to be a certain way, and for people to be a certain way. So he kept doing the same things over and over that weren't working, with faith that they would if he just kept at it long enough.

All these things, Fezziwig surmised, is what made Rood snap when given the blood lust excuse to do so. That vampire blood passed down directly from the king of the fallen angels to Fezziwig to Rood, changing Rood more deeply than any other person whom Fezziwig had turned before.

The change was immediate and gruesome.

Usually his new vampire spawns spent weeks frightened, hungry, and begging for Fezziwig's help to survive.

But Rood didn't seek Fezziwig's advice. He tried to kill him, instead, managing to knock the ancient vampire unconscious with an oak branch. He then went back to his little cabin on his little farm. His wife and kids were waiting for him to bring home a loaf of bread or some carrots (*we do not eat meat, children, we do not shed innocent blood! Thou shalt NOT kill!*) and he slaughtered them.

He started with his wife, sinking his newly grown fangs into her skull.

He didn't know why he chose her skull.

Didn't vampires drink from the neck?

Maybe they did.

But his fangs were razor sharp and hard as stone. His body surged with strength and power. He hated that fat cow more than anything he could think of. So he woke her up, told her it was time to *eat*, and watched her eyes light up when he said it was feeding time.

But he wasn't talking about food for *them*.

He was talking about food for himself.

He had yet to taste blood. But he *knew* it would be delightful. So he sunk his 6-inch fangs – which he could make grow at will (and shrink back to normal tooth size after) – down to his chin, into her head.

Blood sprayed out.

He threw his head back and laughed as she screamed.

He couldn't help it.

What fun!

What deliciously unclean *fun!*

He then watched – with an erection forming in his pants, something he hadn't had since the night their last child had been conceived five years earlier – the life leave her eyes. Her last thoughts were pure horror at what her husband had become and what he'd do to the *children*. After the light left her eyes and she gave up the ghost, he raped her dead body and drank deeply from her jugular.

As he raped her body and drank her blood, he thought about how his wife was fat, but still a good woman.

She was always a good mother, too,

And she was an especially good Christian.

He'd never had such an *orgasm* before.

The blood tasted so refreshing. It was dry and *spicy* – just like the finely aged Italian wine he had once tasted. He never forgot how wonderful that wine was. He drank his wife's blood until his belly was so bloated he felt it'd burst. He then climbed into bed next to her and kicked her to the floor. He was so strong he effortlessly moved the 300-pound corpse.

He needed to burp.

He was still hungry – still wanted to *feed* – but he needed to burp, first. Otherwise he'd throw up his meal. And what a *waste* that would be.

Finally, after a few minutes, he burped.

Ah! It felt so *good*.

He then felt the need to urinate and relieved himself outside. The urine was stained red from his meal. It reminded him of the time when he and his family ate nothing but beets from the garden for two weeks during a food shortage. His whole family had blood-red urine. As he finished pissing, he sensed the last few drops of his lingering humanity leave with the last few drops of lingering piss in his bladder.

It seemed so... *poetic*.

He walked back inside, locked the door, and swallowed the key. His children were trapped inside with him. There would be no hope of escape. No possibility of rescue. Before he was done with them, they would beg him for the sweet release of death.

He tortured, slaughtered, and fed on his children one-by-one. Oh how *delicious* their blood tasted! How *musical* their screams sounded! How *delightful* the skin he messily peeled off them smelled. He skinned their little bodies alive, one strip at a time.

There was less blood than his fat wife had. But their blood tasted just as good even though it was different. Less spicy, but more *rich*.

He quite liked being a vampire. He quite liked the taste of child blood and the sound of peeling skin off. That night the Pastor died.

Only the Vampire was left.

- 4 -

Fezziwig lost track of Rood after that night but saw his atrocities.

Rood was insane with evil.

He had no self-control – and he had urges and an appetite for killing Fezziwig had never even imagined, much less seen, all the centuries he'd been alive. Fezziwig hunted the countryside for Rood, always a day or two behind. Most newly turned vampires take years – sometimes *decades* – to learn and master their newfound powers, abilities, and appetites.

But Rood was different.

It was like he had been "prepared" for the change.

It was like he'd secretly – in the deepest recesses of his mind – dreamed of having the power to let loose. To not be bound by these silly rules in his silly religion telling him to do silly things like turn the other cheek and pray for his enemies, and if someone steals your coat give him your *shirt*, too. Rood followed those rules to the letter and it caused him and his family to suffer day after day – people stealing money from the church, taking advantage of his generosity, never changing.

They lived like the meek and ate like the poor.

They refused to fight or engage in any conflict.

Violence was forbidden.

He didn't even allow himself to defend his wife when they were robbed and a band of criminals he'd given shelter to not a week earlier groped and fondled her pussy and breasts. Instead of fighting or standing up to them, he refused to participate in violence. *"At least they didn't* violate *you honey, praise God!"* he told her. Of course, he knew the only reason they didn't fuck her was because she was so fat. Not that he was going to tell her that. Such was his fear of women when he was human.

Rood and his family were "good" people.

Nice people.

Starving people.

Taken advantage of people.

And Rory Rood told himself that was how it should be. That was the way his mentor – another self-proclaimed Christian pacifist – told him to live.

That was the way he would live, too.

And so would his family.

And they would *like* it.

Because that was God's way, after all.

Fezziwig knew Rood had to be put down like a foaming-at-the-mouth dog. As Fezziwig followed Rood's carnage across the land he noticed the evil vampire's appetite – his *palate* – started to change from preferring children's blood to a special kind of blood:

Holy men blood.

Pastors, priests, nuns, deacons... anyone who lived in, worked at, or attended a church. Anyone he heard praying outside their bedroom windows at night... anyone with a Bible on their bookshelf. He traveled from church to church, viciously attacking anyone he could find and drinking their blood. He raped wives in front of their husbands. He butchered children and forced their parents to watch. He understood why his wife's blood tasted so good. She was a devout and obedient Christian – and that was a very appetizing seasoning.

Rood went from one church to the next. Each time he sampled and drank the holy men and women inside. It was like an unholy wine-tasting tour. Except, instead of tasting wines, he tasted the *blood* of holy men and women who served God. Many of his victims prayed for the vampire's salvation even as it *feasted* on their families.

Rood also noticed their blood tasted differently depending on how strong their faith was. He would learn of the dark secrets certain church leaders had before attacking them. Like the Deacon who molested his own children – his blood tasted flat, watered-down, and *bland*. While the fire & brimstone preachers who truly loved God and wanted to serve Him... their blood tasted like the most finely aged and cared for wine. The finish lingered in his mouth for hours and made him crave more. So he skipped going after the bad church folk and focused on the good ones. *So much for God counting the very hairs of your head, and valuing you more than the sparrows*, he would mock as he desecrated their families.

The LORD told Fezziwig just before the flood waters wiped out the world not to go down that route again as he once had. To not give in to those evil and depraved base urges, even if he sometimes wanted to, he knew the consequences of doing so. And he never did after that.

But that didn't stop his spawns from doing so.

And in this case, the only good thing about Rood's sloppy atrocities was, it allowed Fezziwig to more easily track him.

His killings had a pattern.

And it would only be a matter of time before Fezziwig found him.

- 5 -

When Fezziwig caught up to Rood, the evil, God-hating vampire had found a concubine that was almost as diabolical as he was.

Her name was Mara Vladislas.

She was originally from Transylvania. And she had sought out Rood *wanting* to be his concubine. She heard all the vampire tales in her homeland and wanted to become one.

(Fezziwig knew he was to blame for Transylvanian vampire lore. He was, after all, the one who originally turned Vlad the Impaler into a vampire, thinking he would turn kings into vampires, and then thereby control those kingdoms as a kind of "puppet master." It never worked out that way due to those kings and rulers getting so power drunk, or being assassinated by Predators.)

Mara found Rood and begged him to turn her, make her his concubine, and promised to do whatever he wanted.

Rood inspected her over. She had a spectacular pair of breasts. She had no open sores, both ears, and still had all her teeth. She was also the most beautiful woman he'd ever seen.

He debated in his mind whether to kill her or turn her. Normally he'd have smitten any woman for having the audacity to approach him at all. He did the hunting, he was not the hunted. But she had a look about her. A *familiar* look that reminded him of his mother.

Rood's mother was a cruel, cold woman. She never showed Rood affection or love and openly despised him. The town they lived in suspected she had killed one of her children after it'd been born with the palsy. Nobody could prove it. But it only took one look into her empty, soulless eyes to know something was not "right" with her.

And so it was with Mara.

She also hated the Christian church as much as Rood did.

She told Rood all the evil acts she did in her hometown church's secret chambers: Seducing priests and having orgies in the pews. Drinking human blood at the altar. Sacrificing stolen babies and children to foreign gods and demons such as Azazel, Dagon, Baal, Ashtaroth, Chemosh, Hadad, Molech, Milcom, Tammuz, Marduk, Ishtar, and the devil. She also beheaded statues of the saints, and replaced them with stone-carved heads of demons and devils.

All that helped her case with Rood.

But they didn't sell her on him.

What sold him was she possessed his mother's eyes. Yes, she would make an excellent concubine. So Rood turned her.

Mara became his partner in crime – drinking the blood of holy men, setting churches on fire, and profaning God at every turn. Mara taught Rood the art and craft of skinning people alive. He had tried so many times to get it right. It was always so *messy* when he did it. And the victims died too soon. But she knew how to keep the victims alive for weeks, cutting off their eyelids so they couldn't look away. She kept them in constant agony, screaming, and yelling. The tormented screams sexually excited the two vampires. While they let their victims sit in agony from having the skins peeled off their bodies, the vampires had their unholy sex and bloodletting acts right in front of their lidless eyes.

Mara had been a monster even before she was a vampire.

Fezziwig later found out, as he tortured Mara for all this information about her and Rood's lives, that she had killed over 19 people in Transylvania – skinning them alive, too.

She was a master at skinning with a rusty straight blade. That was her trademark.

It was a lost art she mostly learned when visiting South America and studying the ancient Aztec ways of performing human sacrifice. Using a rusty razor was her original contribution to the art.

When Rood saw Mara knew the craft of skinning he became *her* student. He would break into a church, wait for a nun or pastor or priest to come in, and practice on them all night until the sun came up. And while the sun was up, he'd let them suffer in their pains, taking great care they'd still be alive the next night when he awoke.

He'd peel off one strip of skin at a time. He'd do it slowly, and in a way where all the nerves would scream and howl. Oh how he *loved* their screams!

He would kiss and bite Mara's neck as he tore skin off his victim with the rusty razor. Sometimes they would kidnap several holy people and make them have perverted sex with each other and drink each other's blood. The two vampires got aroused by watching these gruesome acts. The fear and horror was like a *drug* to them. The more they experienced it, the more they needed it, and the more their evil grew.

Fezziwig finally caught Mara in a church in the middle of nowhere in the land that would one day be called Illinois – near a big wood next to a giant quicksand pit. It was as strange seeing a church in the middle of nowhere as it was to see the quicksand.

Who built that church?

Fezziwig did not know. But the architecture looked French.

Rood was gone that night – no doubt hunting on his own, maybe skinning someone in another church. Fezziwig was far more powerful than Mara and easily captured her. He tortured her for hours for information.

He learned all about Rood's past. He learned all about her past. And he learned all about the sick, evil things they'd both been up to.

Fezziwig got everything he could from her, promising to let her go (*"you're not the one I want to kill..."*) then proceeded to stake her through the heart, behead her, stuff her mouth with garlic, and burn her with fire. He tossed her head and ashes and remains in the quicksand in a big sack.

That was when, for the first time in centuries, Fezziwig heard the voice of the LORD. He hadn't heard it since Noah's flood, when the LORD told him how to survive it. Fezziwig didn't know why the LORD spared him. Perhaps the LORD would use him some day?

Whatever the case, the voice was there.

That voice Fezziwig had to obey.

It was *audible*, but still in his head, like someone whispering something behind a crack in a door and into his mind. *What were the odds of Fezziwig hearing The LORD's voice, at this spot, right now?*

The LORD was telling him something.

What was the word? It sounded like "prison." Fezziwig couldn't quite understand it. But it was the LORD's voice. Of that there was no doubt.

Fezziwig interpreted the cryptic command as this was a special place – and was to be a prison for vampires he killed. He decided he would build a town around this church and the quicksand pit. Since the LORD spoke to him there, Fezziwig considered it *holy* ground. He would hunt down the other vampires he'd created and the ones they'd created and the ones they'd created. He would stake, behead, stuff their mouths with garlic, and toss their remains in the quicksand *prison* the LORD whispered to him.

He started with tossing Mara's remains in.

Rood would be next.

Then, all his other vampire spawns would join them.

- 6 -

Fezziwig waited for Rood to return.

He figured he and Mara had some kind of secret rendezvous figured out. Either he was supposed to meet her in the church or somewhere else. But eventually he'd come looking for her. Vampires had a very special pair bond when they took a new concubine and turned her into a vampire. It was for life and unbreakable. It was one reason Fezziwig never turned any of his concubines. He didn't want the attachment. He had enough problems without having to add dealing with a lifelong woman to the mix.

But Rood and Mara had an especially strong bond even for vampires. It was forged in blood, dark demonic religion, and passion. And there was no way Rood would not come for her.

Rood showed up three nights later.

He flew in through the church window in bat form.

"Concubine, where are you? You'd better not be skinning meat *without* me," Rood said as he transformed back into a vampire.

Fezziwig watched from the church rafters as a bat. He wanted to study his adversary before attacking. He'd never heard of a vampire as powerful as Rood. Rood was also taller than other vampires. He was stronger and more cunning. Fezziwig wondered if Rood was even stronger than himself.

Rood would no doubt suspect a trap.

He sniffed the air. A vampire knows his concubine's scent. He also knows the scent of her fear – which still befouled the air from when Fezziwig caught, tortured, and killed Mara.

Rood's senses were at full strength.

He could sense everything in the church – every sound, smell, movement, taste, and even *thought*. Something else was in there with him. Something as strong as himself. Rood had come across several different Nephilim monsters during his killing sprees; they weren't just vampires, but other evil things, too.

Like chimeras, gorgons, succubus, djinn, demonic spirits of other monsters he killed, gargoyles, ghouls, werewolves, golems, hell hounds, harpies, imps, wraiths, minotaurs, animated skeletons, ogres, satyrs, witches, trolls, wights, skin walkers, and even a fallen angel who was tormenting a family with visions of strange, gray colored beings with huge eyes who claimed to come from the heavens.

Some of these beings he fought.

Some he avoided.

And some he joined up with – a mutual love of killing holy men.

He'd also come across a Predator, too, and killed him by shoving his head into water and drowning him. He wanted to drink the Predator's blood. But it smelled disgusting. It was so bad; he didn't even bother tasting it. Instead, he did to the Predator what it had meant to do to him: staked him through the heart, cut off his head, stuffed garlic down his throat, and set him on fire. There was a funny kind of irony to that, Rood thought.

But this presence was no Predator. It was another vampire.

Rood was too startled to react.

And unfortunately for Rood, his senses and speed and strength were not at that time a match for Fezziwig who landed on Rood's face in bat form, bit out his left eye, and then flew into Rood's mouth as he screamed in pain. Rood choked as Fezziwig made his way down his throat.

And in a flash of pain, Fezziwig turned into his full vampire form inside Rood's stomach, just as he'd done to the owl that ate him as a bat. As Fezziwig turned into his vampire form, Rood's torso ripped wide open and his head popped off and onto the ground. Fezziwig was covered in Rood's blood and veins and entrails. He wasted no time staking what was left of the heart in the still writhing torso, stuffing garlic in the decapitated head's mouth, and burning the body.

Fezziwig gathered the remains and made his way to the quicksand pit where he tossed it in right next to Mara's remains, along the bank next to the edge of the pit.

He watched it sink before leaving.

- 7 -

That was when Fezziwig made the final decision there could be no other vampires. He wasn't sure he wanted to purge them all from the earth while hunting Rood. He still thought he might not have to do the deed. He hated the idea of destroying his spawns… but they were not his *literal* children, not his flesh, even if they had his blood.

So after Rood's death he knew they *all* had to die, every last one of them. They were too big a threat to his existence.

It was much better to let the world think vampires were extinct and he was dead. That would throw off any Predators on his trail. It would make the world forget about vampires altogether. Fezziwig could live a nice, simple life with his concubines. He wouldn't have to worry about being hunted or killed or having to take the heat for what other vampires did.

So he got busy hunting and purging vampires. One after the other he went after them. Thankfully, none were as strong or evil or powerful as Rood. They were mostly easy pickings. And they were all a lot easier to track, too.

Fezziwig hunted and killed over 700 vampires during the next 200 years. He tossed their burned remains and garlic mouth stuffed heads into the quicksand. When he found the last one – a particularly nasty woman vampire – in London, England, he had his concubine take a picture of him holding its severed head. The picture was later stolen from him.

Fezziwig built Belasco around that church and put a fence around the quicksand. He found a holy man and had the quicksand – which has water inside it – blessed so it was holy water-mingled. That would make sure any vampires inside stayed dead and couldn't be resurrected. Even if some shaman or dark force was able to give the dead vampire remains life again, they would die again just as quickly from the acid-like water in the sand. He returned sometimes, to see if the voice of the LORD could be heard but never heard anything.

Eventually, Fezziwig stopped going back, and decided he had enough of it all.

He went to Alaska where he could live in peace with his concubines, returning to Belasco only every few decades to make sure everything was still in place.

Until now.

Now, somehow, Rood was back. He was up to something, too. The LORD told him so. The LORD also told Fezziwig what to do – *both* his missions – when he got to Belasco, and to seek the help of the Predator who was already there.

We'll see if this little faggot Predator can help, Fezziwig thought, as he landed in Belasco just before dawn. He found a dark tree hole devoid of sunlight to lay in and went to sleep, ready to awaken and fulfill his mission at sundown.

7

HIDE AND STINK

*"Clowns to the left of me. Jokers to the right. Here I am
stuck in the middle with you."*

- Stealers Wheel
Stuck in the Middle with You

- 1 -

Azriel awoke at sunset to his danger "warning bell" rage stirring in his gut.

The sun was going down and he realized he must have been far more exhausted than he thought to have slept several hours away. He was still tired and groggy. And for the first few seconds he didn't realize where he even was. His body was a tangle of aches, raw nerves, and bruises from the night before and his encounter in Pastor Shane's panic room.

"Idiot, letting yourself go like this," he said aloud, nursing a bruise on top of his head. For the past three years something inside him warned him to not let his body go soft.

To not drink so much beer and booze and wine.

To not eat all those Hot Tamales candy and ice cream.

To not drink all that soda pop.

To not consume so many milkshakes.

To not let himself get so out of shape.

And, to never let his guard down.

It was so much easier to forget about all the monsters. To dive into his new career. To date as many women as he could. To eat, drink, and be irresponsible. All he had wanted to do was forget his memories of the evil and blood and guts and carnage he'd seen. To forget the night his would-be girlfriend Kerry Ditzler and his mother and his best friend were desecrated by Chief Rawger. To forget how he had to destroy everyone in town. But those memories were flooding back into his mind, fueling the instinct-triggered rage already burning inside him with the monsters on his tail, and the realization that his grandmother, his own flesh and blood (*or, so she said...*), betrayed him.

Azriel had collapsed deep into the Belasco Woods. It was a trail he'd hoped none of them would know about. It'd been hours since he escaped and he assumed Granny had been looking for him. Or perhaps they were waiting until the sun went down so the vampires could join the hunt. He felt them approaching, sensed their presence, and practically smelled their

81

evil.

How far away were they?

A hundred yards?

Fifty yards?

Ten yards?

He got up and started running without even brushing the leaves and dirt off his pants and shirt. He remembered where he was. He was on the same trail he'd been when he was hunting monsters with Kerry Ditzler and Marvin Worely the day of the Belasco Woods Massacre. They didn't find any monsters that day. But they did get attacked by a pack of blood-thirsty dogs that Azriel butchered.

It was deja-vu for Azriel Creed. This whole experience was just that. Hadn't he done this dance before? The story and stage were the same as last time. Only the *monsters* changed.

When he could run no more, his heart feeling as if it were nearly ready to give out, he stopped by a familiar looking tree. He was in the same spot ten miles into the forest where he'd killed those foaming-at-the-mouth dogs.

Was it just coincidence?

Or was something *guiding* him?

He'd have to think about that another time. These woods had saved his life twice before. With any luck, they would do so again...

- 2 -

Azriel dropped to his knees dry heaving from exhaustion. His stomach ached and throbbed with each breath.

How was he supposed to fight like this?

His balls tightened and his throat watered – the usual precedent to puking from exhaustion. He let himself vomit. His last full meal was with Mina the night before, prior to impaling her iPhone with his steak knife. He had eaten two helpings of pasta, and knocked back a large Pepsi and four LandShark beers when he finally couldn't stand Mina's rudeness and made them leave. Azriel binged in everything he did – working, playing, fighting, drinking, and especially eating. His appetite for sugar and junk food and beer was ferocious.

As Azriel caught his breath he stood up and spat out any leftover vomit still in his mouth.

He could hear his pursuers coming. Their voices weren't far off. They'd be on him soon.

Moment of truth, Azriel.

Do you take a stand here and fight?

Probably get yourself killed?

You might be able to take down the tall vampire chick with the ginormous tits. Although there is something about her. About the way she stood, the look in her eye... she was far more powerful than the other vampires last night. Especially the way she tossed you through the thick oak door like a rag doll.

There's Granny, too, the perverted traitor lying bitch.

She's capable of all the same things you are. Except she's in far better shape and also a better fighter. She's brutal, too. She says you're the most powerful Predator she's seen. If that's true then why can't you run 100 yards without tossing your dinner...?

Azriel barely remembered how he defeated all those were-monsters in Chicago. It was like a haze of pure instinct. And it damn near killed him from exhaustion. He would need to tap into that rage again if he wanted to live.

The were-monsters.

Why did Granny take him there? If her goal was to betray Azriel, she could have killed him or let him get killed by the vampires. Why *test* him? Was she on the fence about betraying him? Maybe she wanted to take his side instead and then changed her mind last minute? He'd figure that out later. He'd put his foot on her wrinkled neck and force her to tell him... right before ripping her ugly head clean off.

Good, Dumb Az, he thought. *Or maybe, Fat Az is more appropriate now. Better let that anger and rage come flowing back. You're gonna* need *it.*

Yes, he would need it. He would need all the help he could get. And the woods... those evil woods where so many people (*an entire town!*) had died at his hands (or was it his *mind?*)... the legends and stories of all the other people who had died there over the years – would provide a great handicap.

Next stop: The quicksand pit.

Azriel formulated an attack plan in his tired mind. It was a desperate plan. It would require his attackers to underestimate him. But if it worked, he could kill them.

He heard Granny and the Jessica Rabbit vampire chick coming. Granny's cackling and Jessica Rabbit vampire chick's deep Eastern European accent were unmistakable.

But... there was also something *else*. Another presence. Someone or *something* had joined their hunt. It was evil and powerful.

And strong.

Was it Rood?

They were so loud. They were not even trying to be stealthy.

They're arrogant. Good. Follow me to the quicksand, bitches. Get cozy with your new grave site... you're going to be here a while.

- 3 -

Azriel ran for the quicksand pit, ignoring the cramp in his side and the fact his heart felt as though it were going to beat right out of his chest. His legs were burning and his ankles ached. If he didn't know better, he would have thought his spine might even be a bit *twisted*. But how would he be able to run if that were the case?

One thing was clear: If he somehow lived through today, he'd definitely feel it tomorrow.

Azriel saw the 10-foot tall fence surrounding the quicksand pit with the barbed wire and he picked up his pace.

His plan was simple: he'd find a spot with a firm rock or tree branch near the surface, tie his belt (which he wore purely for show – his waist was too large to need a belt and he only used the first notch) around it. He'd hide in the quicksand with his head just above the sand from the nose up so he could breathe. When they walked by him, he would do what the vampires did to him and Mina in the alley: grab their ankles and yank them in.

Then, he'd hold them under and let them sink to the bottom. Problem solved.

It was a crazy plan. But what alternative was there?

He came upon the fence and stopped about ten yards away. He spared a few seconds to look back to see if they were coming.

They weren't. He could hear them in the distance, but not see them.

That means they can't see me yet.

Maybe God doesn't hate me as much as I thought...

Azriel couldn't see them, but he could still feel their presence.

Especially the new one.

It's gotta be Rood...

He would soon find out who it was, since they would be upon him. If his plan was to work he'd have to be hiding by the time they got there, and hope they were walking right next to each other. He dug his feet into the ground, ignored the sharp cramp in his side, sprinted as fast as he could towards the fence, and jumped.

He barely cleared it.

When he landed on the other side he tumbled to the ground in a clumsy summersault that made his spine feel even more twisted.

Balls!

My left shoe –

He looked back and saw his shoe caught on the barbed wire.

Unless they're blind and stupid they'll see it.

Azriel saw them – just dark figures, not quite fully in sight, which meant neither was he – coming from the woods towards the fence. If he was going to pull off his plan, he'd have to leave the shoe and hope they didn't see it. Part of him wanted to stand and fight and feed the hot, growing rage inside him. He wanted to take these bitches *down*. But the thinking side of his brain said to be patient. He didn't know exactly what he was up against.

The Jessica Rabbit vampire was powerful.

Granny was nobody to trifle with, either.

And the other thing was surely stronger than them both.

So really, there was no choice.

Into the quicksand he'd go.

- 4 -

Azriel's plan instantly dissolved when he stood up and turned around to find a spot in the quicksand to hide. The building anger and rage was replaced by a new feeling:

Surprise.

There *was* no quicksand anymore. The pit was there. But there was barely any *sand* left.

Whatever made Azriel's body strong and adaptable and fast also gave him tremendous night vision when under stress. It didn't seem to work as well when he was calm. But even without the bright moon beaming its light down through the surrounding trees he could see the remains of skeletons (*there must be hundreds of them!*) and skulls and garbage and debris people had tossed over the fence into the pit over the years. The pit's center contained an especially large pile of skeletons, bones, and skulls... as well as other debris. Wherever the quicksand was going, that seemed to be the drain, and most of the skeletons had gathered there from the suction.

So many bodies of people had been disposed of in the pit. Everyone in Belasco knew it. The police were often quoted saying they suspected many an unsolved murder case could be closed if they were to make that quicksand disappear.

No wonder the place felt evil. No wonder people avoided it even though it was a famous landmark. Where else was there a giant quicksand lake like that in the world? The billboards on Route 57 advertised it as the world's biggest quicksand pit. A few people would stop in, but hardly anyone stayed.

Belasco was too creepy. What was there to see, anyway? It gave anyone who came near it a bad feeling. People who visited and lived there sometimes said they felt like they were being *watched* – observed by something that wanted to make that quicksand pit their new home.

Azriel made a few contributions to the pit, too: Specifically the two big safes and three small safes containing Chief Rawger's remains and head, as well as the original zombie head, and Finius' head and remains.

Finius.

He remembered Finius the most since his was the last one he dumped in there just a year earlier. That was mere days after he *fed* Finius to the original zombie head. It was disgusting.

It took weeks to get the smell and stains out of the apartment. The neighbors complained. Even the health inspector made a visit. It was worth it to rid the planet of that son of a bitch who betrayed Pastor Shane and engineered the zombie threat in the first place.

More family treachery now appears in Belasco. First it was Finius betraying his distant cousin. Today it was Granny betraying her grandson. Again, he thought, the story was the same. Only the *monsters* changed.

After defeating Finius, Azriel drove down to Belasco the next day with the safes. The original zombie head kept clicking its teeth – always chomping, always hungry, always wanting to *feed*. Azriel came right to this pit. The town was completely empty (who would want to come back and live here?) And, in another twist of irony not lost on him, he came to the *exact* spot he was now standing. He tossed them in the quicksand never to be seen again.

Except they were being seen again. Now. Azriel saw the two big safes housing Finius and Rawger's body remains that weren't totally digested (mostly bones and gristle), and the three small safes with all their heads. Five safes. All sealed tight, and supposedly uncrackable.

Except...

Two of the safes – a big and a small one – looked like they were ajar. It was hard to tell from a distance. Now that Azriel thought about it, when he returned last year, the quicksand pit *did* seem a bit lower. But he figured that was just from the explosion in the woods rattling the ground and tossing some of it up and out. Had it been draining this whole time?

Azriel temporarily forgot about his pursuers. If the zombies had escaped again the whole world really was screwed. He'd have two enemies – both vampires and zombies.

Vampires to left of me, zombies to the right, here I am stuck in the middle with you, Dumb Az.

Azriel slid down the slope into the pit. It was at least a hundred feet deep to the bottom, and was shaped like a gravel pit. He had to slide through residual patches of toe-deep quicksand to reach the bottom. He could hear voices from the fence area. He could hear the cackle which obviously belonged to Granny. He could hear the Eastern European-accented voice that belonged to the busty Jessica Rabbit vampire chick. And a man's voice which, when it spoke, was followed by a *tooting* noise that reminded Azriel of the Popeye cartoons whenever Popeye tooted on his pipe.

It was a deep, dark, sinister voice.

It *crackled* with evil.

The mere echo of it instantly triggered Azriel's inborn hatred of all things monster.

But he ignored that for now. He was far more interested in the safes. Or, rather, what had *escaped* from them.

- 5 -

Azriel couldn't be totally sure which of the zombies the cracked-open safes belonged to.

But, they were definitely open.

And, empty.

Was it Rawger? Or Finius? Or maybe either Rawger's or Finius's body, but the original zombie head?

If the original zombie head saw a decapitated zombie body that belonged to someone else, could he attach to it? Was that even possible? Was anything not possible at this point?

But who could have opened them?

All Azriel knew for sure was one of the zombies was on the loose. There was nobody to eat in Belasco. But that wouldn't stop him (whichever zombie it was) for long. Azriel remembered how having their heads and their bodies in close proximity, even those bodies that were destroyed, would let the more powerful ones resurrect themselves.

Vampires *and* zombies?

The three pursuers were now over the fence.

They didn't bother jumping that fence. One of them – the one Azriel assumed was Rood – ripped it right out of the ground and tossed part of it into the pit, damn near hitting him.

What now, tough guy?

Fight?

Hide?

Not enough quicksand left for that.

Wait… yes, you can *hide…*

Azriel knew they'd be looking down upon him in a few seconds. He took a deep breath, climbed into the big safe, and closed the door as much as he could without locking himself inside.

- 6 -

Even with his accentuated senses Azriel couldn't hear through the safe.

He could still feel the presence – that evil, *dark* presence – of the two things walking with his traitor grandma, as they made their way down into the pit. He heard a muffled cackle here, a displeased voice there. A weird "tooting" sound, too.

Even worse than the anticipation of being found was the *smell*.

It was the worst smell he'd ever encountered. It was even worse than the smells he experienced while chained up in Rawger's jail, with all the leftover dead bodies and carcasses and blood and guts and entrails around him. Because of his large belly and the way he was positioned inside, Azriel couldn't even cover his nose. The fumes wafted into his nostrils and he wanted to *puke*. It'd be poetic justice if he did. All those times as a kid in church when he farted during Pastor Shane's sermons just to get a rise out of people came back to haunt him.

The evil presence got closer with each passing moment.

They may have noticed the safes before today. Did they know what was inside? Granny probably did. Maybe they opened them up?

Azriel hoped his safe door was closed enough where they wouldn't notice it being slightly cracked. He wished he could crack it even more just to let some of the smell out. But he dare not.

A thought occurred to him: He knew if he can sense them, then they can surely sense him. *Balls!* He hadn't considered that. He knew they were standing right by his safe now. He could make out their words a little more clearly. It sounded like they were deciding which direction Azriel ran. They saw his shoe, knew he was nearby, and couldn't have gone far.

"Go that way, hag," said the dark voice. "We'll check over here – it stretches far and Mara and I can avoid the sandy spots so we don't *burn*."

"Okey-dokey, Mr. Skipper."

"*Skipper!*" – Azriel heard that name referenced by the vampires in Chicago.

Azriel felt the evil presences walk away a bit.

Maybe this was working.

Azriel didn't know for sure, but he hoped they were moving far away from him. Then he would have time to plot and plan his attack. He couldn't leave Belasco now without taking care of the vampire menace any more than he could have left Belasco before without taking care of the zombie menace.

Azriel waited for as long as he could handle the stench inside the safe to crack the door open a little more to see what was going on. He could still feel their presence – dark, evil, creating an ongoing pit in his stomach. It made him angry.

But he couldn't hear them.

No voices.

No tooting noise.

He opened it a little more.

It felt good to air the stinking safe out. He opened it a little more... until, finally, he thought it safe to open it all the way. He still felt them nearby – close. But he had to risk it. When he opened the door he would be able to see which way they all went by their footprints. As Azriel climbed out, his eyes looking at the ground, he felt a strong pair of hands grab him by the shoulders, and a fist slam him across his right temple.

Blood dripped into his eye.

"Yoo-hoo, Azriel!"

It was the dark voice.

Azriel stared up at an unusually tall figure with a face that had two long fangs, dark gray skin, a patch over its right eye, and jet black hair underneath what looked like a ship captain's hat. It also had a corncob pipe in its mouth. The thing blew into it and that Popeye tooting sound came out.

"Welcome aboard the SS Rood. It's a swell ship for the skipper, but a hell ship for the *crew*."

The evil vampire's smile wrapped around the pipe handle.

It was creepy, and sinister, and amusing all at once.

Toot!

- 7 -

Azriel didn't know if it was a joke or real.

Rood was certainly nothing like he was expecting. Yes, it was big and strong and powerful looking. Its one eye glowed red like Azriel's did. Its smile was devious and sinister. Its teeth were sharp.

But that pipe that poked out of the side of his mouth?

And that ship captain's hat?

What the fuck was that about?

Azriel didn't have a lot of time to process it.

Even as the thing wailed on his face and body and legs and back... moving so fast Azriel could barely even see its fists... it would periodically blow on that stupid pipe which sounded like it was rigged so it sounded like a ship horn. Azriel would have laughed if he wasn't getting his ass kicked – spitting up blood and sucking in air from having the wind knocked out of him.

Granny and the Jessica Rabbit vampire stood and watched, laughing and cackling as the monster known as Rood – "The Skipper" – beat on Azriel.

Azriel tried fighting back.

He tapped into all the rage he could muster. But his body was too exhausted. It was as if he'd blown his anger load on the were-monsters. At best he was able to block a punch with his arm or dodge a kick to his stomach.

The fight wasn't even close. All that rage Azriel had... all the power (unless that line about him being the most powerful Predator Granny had ever seen was just *bullshit*, to inflate his ego and make him easier pickings)... and he couldn't even land a single punch against this silly looking vampire.

Rood was way stronger than Azriel. Way faster. Way more cunning and ruthless and quick.

Azriel felt his bones breaking, his insides bleeding, blood shot out of his mouth in spurts as the thing pummeled him. It was a lot like when Todd Rawger and Leo Gomez beat him to what they thought was death.

Except this was far worse. And more *painful*. The beating hurt more... and it lasted longer... and this time, Azriel didn't black out. Whatever it was that made his body hard to kill, didn't seem to let him get out of an ass kicking that easily.

"You need an attitude adjustment, my friend." said Rood as he grabbed Azriel's neck and lifted him off the ground. His hand started to crush Azriel's throat. "Don't you worry, though. Your Captain will *help* with that. We run a *tight* ship around here!"

Rood used his free hand to sock Azriel in the face. Azriel felt himself losing consciousness.

Death? Probably.

Hey, Azriel, you gave it a good run.

You did what you could.

You stopped the zombies at least.

Or did you?

No, you didn't.

One escaped.

And what was it Granny said about you starting this? You being responsible *for the vampires coming back? She never did explain that.*

No matter.

Azriel realized he would soon be dead, and it wouldn't be his problem. He could only hope God would find some room in his heart to forgive him for being *what* he is. Pastor Shane called him and his Predator kind an *abomination*.

Unclean.

There's probably a special *spot reserved in hell for me...*

The vampire continued to punch Azriel. It hated the boy in ways not even Chief Rawger did. When Rawger kicked his ass it was more of a natural hate – like the hate between a mongoose and a cobra, as Pastor Shane described it. This was different. This was the hate of someone who hated Azriel just for *breathing*.

Azriel's fat belly quivered from all the blows to his face and body. His eyes and mouth and nose gushed blood. It was almost over.

Just as he could feel his life slipping away into unconsciousness – the pounding suddenly stopped. Azriel could barely see out of either eye. Both were nearly swollen shut. But he could hear everything just fine.

He heard a flapping sound followed by a cranky old man's voice. The voice reminded him of a pissed off old World War 2 veteran who told him and his friend Marvin Worely to get off his *lawn* when they tried cutting through his yard.

"I know you!" said the Jessica Rabbit vampire's voice.

"It's like… it's like… it's like it's my *birthday*," said Rood. "And look! You even came in your birthday *suit* didn't you!"

Rood's pipe tooted.

Granny cackled.

But it was a nervous cackle – forced – as if she was scared.

"Leave that boy alone in the name of the LORD, you faggot," said the cranky voice.

"Your lord tried to control me and lost already, he has no power over me," said Rood. "But you saved me the trouble of finding you. You were a little farther down on my priority list. But I'm glad you're here…" Rood's voice sounded darker, not jolly like when he was beating Azriel.

"He's still alive! How wonderful!" said the Jessica Rabbit vampire.

"Indeed it is wonderful, Mara. Indeed it is," said Rood. "After all, I owe you a killing... Fezziwig."

He tooted his pipe.

8
SAVED BY THE ENEMY

"If Hitler invaded hell, I would at least make positive reference to the devil in the House of Commons."

- Winston Churchill

- 1 -

"Get up you little faggot," said the cranky old man's voice. "Get the *hell* UP!"

Through the dark haze of the beating he just took... where he felt the life slipping out of his body (*so this is what it feels like to die... again – just like last time, only more* painful...) Azriel almost thought it was Todd Rawger handing him another beating in the locker room. But that was dumb.

Todd Rawger was dead. So were the rest of everyone else who cheered on the ass beating that day.

Maybe he was hallucinating? One last trick his brain wanted to play on him before shutting off forever? No such luck.

His wits started coming back when the beating stopped. It didn't take long for his body to start healing itself and regain composure. His body didn't completely heal that fast. But he was able to stand and ball up his battered fists, which had been bruised in several places just seconds prior. His vision focused. His mind cleared.

He processed what was happening: He saw his three attackers fighting someone... *something*... else. It, too, was a vampire. An old, tall, buck-naked vampire with chalk-white, wrinkled flesh and flabby man-boobs.

His face looked familiar.

Where had Azriel seen him before? Oh, yes. It was Anghel Belasco. He'd seen Belasco's photo in Pastor Shane's scrapbook three years ago. But this thing looked older and shorter than the man in the photo (or was he just bent over now?) Like a male version of Granny, but with long, protruding teeth that went almost down to his chin. It also had ridiculous looking and unevenly trimmed facial scruff with patches of longer and shorter hairs.

But Anghel Belasco wasn't attacking Azriel. He was *helping* him. He was fighting Azriel's three would-be killers. And he was asking for Azriel's help.

He's helping you, Dumb Az. So get up. Get. The. Hell. UP!

Azriel stood up. His potbelly poked in and out with each breath. Anger consumed the cobwebs leftover in his brain, and replaced it with clarity. He would fight all these sons of bitches. And, he would *enjoy* it. Oh, yes, even though he was exhausted... and even though it was painful to even *move*... he was going to enjoy this.

- 2 -

"Get in the fight or get back to being dead!" said Fezziwig who, as frail and old as he looked, was so strong, Azriel could literally feel the air move when he threw punches. And the vampire was so fast, he reminded Azriel of how the Agents in the "Matrix" movies moved.

Granny was on Fezziwig's shoulders, cackling, her lidless eyes staring into the back of his horseshoe-patterned hair loss's head. The Jessica Rabbit vampire – who Rood called "Mara" – was slashing and stabbing at Fezziwig with her rusted straight razor. She slashed at his face and mouth and nose and throat. Rood was wailing on Fezziwig's stomach – over and over and over, with the occasional "toot!" sound coming out of his pipe the harder the evil vampire breathed. Rood was in a rage. He hit Fezziwig repeatedly without stopping. With Fezziwig it wasn't just blind hatred from Rood like it was with Azriel. It *was personal.* And the sadistic vampire was enjoying himself.

None of attackers realized Azriel was on his feet.

Fezziwig looked at Azriel as if saying, *"What the hell is taking you so long?"*

Patience, Vampire, thought Azriel. He was getting his sight back. The feeling in his toes and fingers and arms back was returning. He was basking in the anger swelling inside him. But the anger was not for Fezziwig. He was angry at the other three – especially the old cackling one.

He attacked Mara first. She was closest and most vulnerable. In a moment, Azriel was behind her, to the side of Rood who was still punching Fezziwig's stomach. Blood spurted out of Fezziwig's mouth. Azriel kicked Rood in the side of the face, knocking him to the ground. He then put his left hand around Mara's throat and, with his right hand's fingers, gouged her eyes, pressing his thin fingertips in so hard he felt warm, oozing liquid.

Mara screamed and dropped the razor. Azriel pushed as hard as he could into her eyeballs. He dug towards the back of her orbits trying to reach her skull.

What happens if you rip a vampire's eyes out?

Do they grow back?

Guess we'll find out!

Azriel squeezed Mara's neck so hard he felt her larynx crush. She gargled and hacked and reflexively knocked Azriel away from her. Azriel's fingers came out of her eyes making a loud noise that sounded like a cork coming out of a champagne bottle. Blood poured out of Mara's eyes and onto her fingers and hands as she covered her face.

Granny set her lidless gaze on Azriel and jumped from Fezziwig's shoulders right into Azriel's torso, licking her lips and cackling as she punched Azriel's face, and ears, and skull. Her blows were almost as strong and devastating as Rood's.

Balls!

This old bitch can punch!

How can someone so fucking old be so strong?

Azriel's nose shattered and he punched her back, connecting her left lidless eye, knocking her to the ground. Fezziwig and Azriel stood side by side. Mara and Granny regrouped with Rood who was cracking his knuckles and smiling.

"Okay gentlemen," Rood said. "I've got some good news and some bad news. Bad news is, all I can offer you is *pain*. The good news is I got *tons* of it!"

Rood tossed his head back laughing and tooted on his pipe.

- 3 -

Azriel didn't remember much of what happened next.

He went into the same haze of anger and violence he did when he entered the were-monster party. Except, these were not dumbed-down, lazy were-monsters who were clearly not expecting to fight, much less used to fighting Predators. The were-monsters were fighting scared. They fought like they were just trying to not get hurt. They attacked, and were ferocious and powerful, but they lacked the will to want to fight. They were playing to not lose, not playing to win. They were, in their own way, just as fat and out of shape as Azriel was – used to being fed, and not having to hunt. They looked and behaved like aristocrats – people who didn't fight or get their own food, preferring instead to pay others to do those messy tasks for them.

It was the opposite with Rood and his two fiends. They were stronger, faster, and more cunning. They were more skilled and fought "dirty." And, they *liked* it. Unlike the were-monsters, Rood and gang weren't fighting for survival. They were fighting to kill, with a mission and a purpose.

Azriel punched and kicked and tackled and bit and scratched and stomped. He attacked anything in his way. He even accidentally hit Fezziwig – who was taken aback by the rage of the unassuming kid with the belly poking out so much his shirt didn't fit over the hump. But even with all Azriel's rage and brutality... and even with all of Fezziwig's speed and cunning... they were no match for Rood. Rood seemed to have twice the strength, stamina, and speed of both Fezziwig and Azriel combined.

One direct hit from Rood almost took Azriel's head clean off. One kick to the stomach and Fezziwig thought Rood's foot would go straight *through* his spine.

Then there was Mara. Deadly, evil, beautiful, Mara. Her eyes healed within seconds. Jelly-like goo stained her cheeks. She wielded her rusty straight razor like it was *one* with her hand. She cut and hacked and sliced at Azriel and Fezziwig, nearly slicing off their fingers and barely missed cutting out their eyes. Blood sprayed anywhere she decided to slash.

And, of course, there was Granny. Nimble, cackling, so strong she can punch straight through a monster's rib cage and pull their heart *clean* out. Her lidless eyes were always watching. Azriel kept trying to pluck one of her eyes out whenever she got close enough. But she was too fast. Too clever.

They needed to run but Azriel hated the thought of running. But there was no way they could win this fight. Not now, at least.

They would need to get away or die.

- 4 -

Fezziwig was amazed at the boy's strength.

Did this little faggot not understand how *powerful* he was? Did he not know the humming of raw power that pulsated from within him? Why was he holding it back? Or did he just not care enough to learn how to release the terrible energies stored inside his body and mind?

Look at him: fat belly. Out of shape. Wheezing and hacking.

The little faggot was red from exhaustion and punched and kicked without any skill or precision. The LORD didn't warn him about this. The LORD said the Predator could help him complete his mission – *both* missions.

The boy had heart, though. He had determination, too. And he had the burning drive to kill their three attackers, not backing down, and ignoring the gruesome amounts of pain he was enduring, as well as the flabs of cut flesh dangling from his arms, and face, and legs, and gut from Mara's razor. Blood streamed out of every hole on his head – from his ears, nose, and mouth.

And he was clumsy. Almost *comical*. Like a raw newbie swordsman picking up the world's best, sharpest sword and hacking away with it mindlessly, without the faintest idea how to wield it.

Fezziwig needed to get this boy away and hide. They were no match for Rood and his two cronies.

Rood was incredibly powerful somehow. He was dangerous when Fezziwig first found him. Not too bright though, the way Rood let Fezziwig fly into his mouth, down his gullet, and transform to his humanoid form while inside his stomach.

But now?

Rood was taller, stronger, and more *twisted*. But what was with the stupid pipe and ship captain's hat? How was he so strong? How was he even *alive*?

Fezziwig had fought a lot of monsters over the years. But nothing was as powerful as Rood. Rood felt no pain. Fezziwig's blows and Azriel's wild swings barely even fazed Rood. The vampire was hopped up on something strong – and Fezziwig couldn't help but wonder where *he* could get a little of whatever it was, too.

I bet he won't have prostate problems when he's 5,500 years old...

Rood needed to be put down. And it had to be done soon, according to the LORD.

But not here. Not now. Not with the boy being more of a liability than an asset.

- 5 -

"Alright ya' swabs," said Rood, imitating a pirate's voice and tooting on his pipe. He stood over Azriel and Fezziwig's broken bodies. They were spitting up blood and holding broken limbs. Azriel used his hand to keep his guts inside from Mara's razor. "Any last words before I make you walk the plank? Oh, and by 'walk the plank' I mean have Mara peel your flesh off?"

Another toot on that damn pipe.

Azriel wanted to shove it up the smug vampire's ass. Mara stood to Rood's right with Granny to his left.

"Hey you," said Azriel looking at Granny. He was panting hard, and barely able to speak. He looked like he was ready to pass out. His eyes were nearly swollen shut and his shoulder was limp from being dislocated.

"What can I do you for, Sexy," said Granny. "You want one last dip inside my dried up old crusty cunt before they take you to the skinning chamber? I watched her skin a Predators *dick* last time. You can get one last use out of yours before she does the same to you!"

"I want you to know something," Azriel replied, spitting out a mouthful of blood. He figured he was bleeding internally and he kept hearing a loud ringing in his right ear wondering if his eardrum was about to *pop*.

"What's that, Sexy?"

"I'm going to kill *you* first. And then I'm going to put your eyes on a chain, and wear it around my *neck*."

Azriel didn't know why he said that. But as he did, he had the urge to do just as he said. It was an urge so strong it overcame his pain and exhaustion. And with a speed so fast it made even Rood and Fezziwig look slow, he knocked his dislocated shoulder into place by hitting it against the ground, hopped to his feet, snatched the razor out of Mara's hand, and dove right at

Granny. It happened so fast Granny couldn't process how the boy could move like that, with parts of his guts spilling out onto the ground. With his free hand, Azriel grabbed Granny's throat and squeezed as hard as he could. With this other hand, he plunged the razor straight into Granny's chest so hard his fist went right through her. Her heart was impaled on the end of it coming out of her back.

Granny's lidless eyes stared into Azriel's as the life left her body.

Azriel pulled his arm out and made two slashes with the razor, cutting both her eyes out. They plopped to the ground, staring up at him. Her body slumped to the ground next to her eyes.

Before Rood and Mara could get their bearings – they'd never even heard of anything like that before (*"Who IS this boy?"*) – Fezziwig said two words before turning into a bat: "Run, faggot!"

Azriel threw the straight razor as hard as he could right into Rood's eye that wasn't covered by an eye patch. Rood yelled out. The pipe dropped out of his mouth. Apparently the vampire could feel pain, after all.

At least there'll be no fucking toot this time, thought Azriel, as he turned and ran up the side of the pit.

Mara turned to tend Rood as Azriel ran past her. "Go get him Concubine! Get him!" Rood screamed, as he plucked the razor out of his eye. Mara took off and Rood looked at the straight razor. Blood soaked it to the hilt.

"You idiot, you think this eye patch was real? It was just for show!" he yelled. Azriel was running so fast he was already out of hearing range. Rood's eyeball was starting to heal itself. Fezziwig's thought, as he flew away, was he really needed to know Rood's secret. His body didn't heal like that. His body only got older and more useless and more in pain.

But Rood... his body was getting stronger.

And... *younger.*

- 6 -

Azriel followed Fezziwig's bat-shaped form as it flew 15-feet above him.

Fezziwig seemed to know where he was going and Azriel followed. What he knew of Fezziwig was limited. He knew he was an old vampire, and cranky, and wanted to be left alone. Nobody had heard from him in over 100 years according to Pastor Shane. Fezziwig built Belasco and named it after himself. So if there was somewhere to go where they could lay low and not be discovered, chances are Fezziwig knew of such a place.

Or so Azriel hoped.

He didn't trust the vampire. He'd be an idiot to trust anyone again after what Granny did. But he had no choice.

Azriel smiled as he ran, tired and as painful as it was just moving his facial muscles, thinking about how good it felt to kill Granny. He was gasping for breath and a sharp cramp was forming in his side. He'd have to stop soon. He was running on pure adrenaline and anger. But eventually the Hulk would go back in the bottle and turn once again into Bruce Banner. A dumb analogy, he admitted to himself. But it was the only one his frazzled brain could think up.

Fezziwig flew straight for the fountain in the middle of the town square. It was the same place Finius put the original zombie head that started the whole zombie fiasco. The fountain was full of debris and dirt and dust and bird poop. Azriel stopped as Fezziwig turned back into his usual vampire form. He was completely naked. Azriel almost laughed at the vampire's shriveled up balls, huge man boobs, and tiny dick, with his unevenly trimmed *Miami Vice* Sonny Crockett-wannabe facial scruff.

"Quick," Fezziwig said, as he walked into the dry fountain and pushed a small lever on the water spout. A small door opened on the fountain's floor and Fezziwig climbed into it, down a ladder. "Hurry," he hissed.

Azriel hesitated a few seconds. He didn't trust this thing. And he felt that damn monster presence from Fezziwig. But he realized he had little choice. It was either trust this vampire or get killed by the other one. He climbed into the opening and down the ladder; a light brush of wind went past his ear. When his head was fully inside it slowly closed shut with a loud thudding noise.

The ladder went deep into the darkness.

When Azriel got to the bottom he found himself in a small room with some old computer equipment and monitors. Everything was full of dust and cobwebs and mouse turds.

Where were they?

As if the old venerable vampire could read his mind, Fezziwig announced:

"I had this room built in the 1970's so I could spy on the women in town. Yeah, I know, I'm a dirty old man. What of it? Too bad these damn computers never did work properly. We'll be safe here, for now."

- 7 -

Fezziwig flipped some switches and lights came on.

They were in a small room that was no more than 400 square feet. The door to the outside they crawled in was directly above them and Azriel couldn't help but think they were sitting ducks – especially with that evil presence feeling that wouldn't leave. Was something else down here with them? Or maybe Fezziwig triggered the internal warning inside his Predator nervous system? Either way, he knew if Rood and his concubine found them, they'd be trapped with nowhere to go.

"Welcome to the lap of luxury," said Fezziwig sitting on the floor. The lights made his six fingered hands' shadows look like spiders crouched in a corner against the wall.

There was no furniture in the room.

Fezziwig looked as though he hadn't had a meal in days. He also looked like he was in a lot more pain than just what his physical features showed. Fezziwig masked his pain as best he could. He wasn't going to show this kid how much he was hurting. He still needed him, after all, and couldn't have the boy doubting him. The LORD wouldn't like it.

Both of them healed faster than normal – but that didn't make their wounds any less painful.

"Thanks for the rescue," said Azriel. He was sitting against the opposite wall breathing hard. His spine still felt as if it was out of alignment. He twisted his back around. Cracking sounds echoed off the walls.

"That sounded like it *hurt*," said Fezziwig. "I've been in some crazy brawls. But that's as bad as it gets."

"So... you're Anghel Belasco," said Azriel, looking at the deep cut on his navel. It had stopped bleeding and was healing.

"Call me Fezziwig. I know *of* you, but not your name."

"Azriel. Creed. Why did you help me?"

"The LORD told me to."

"The Lord, huh?"

"Did I stutter?"

"Tell the Lord I said *gracias*."

Fezziwig studied Azriel's face for several moments. He did so intently, as if he were trying to look through him.

"What are you staring at?" said Azriel.

"I admire your *work*," said Fezziwig ignoring the question. "Too bad we couldn't meet under better circumstances."

There was another minute of silence.

"Where's my damn concubine when I *need* her," said Fezziwig feeling his ribs. He winced when he touched them. "Starr would slather my body down with Icy Hot. Bring me blood to drink. Draw my bath, and have my slippers and robe standing by. Then she'd massage me... happy finish and all. Dear LORD I could *use* her right about now. You got a concubine, kid?"

"A what?"

"Concubine... a woman."

"She died last night. It was Rood's vampires. Haven't even had a chance to *mourn* her yet. She was turning into a crazy, nagging, cold-hearted bitch, but she didn't deserve to go out like that."

"Crazy is good, my friend."

"Crazy sucks."

"You're wrong. The crazy ones are the most loyal. But they're like bucking hell bitches – you gotta *break* them in first. Once you do, they're yours for life."

"Not American chicks."

Fezziwig chuckled. He took another moment to stare at Azriel, studying his eyes and face. He smiled, then said:

"They're the easiest to control of all. My concubine Starr was a med student. Beautiful. Generous-sized tits. Perfect ass. She had her pick of any man she wanted. She was also nuts, Azriel, *nuts*. Her mind was full of feminist bullshit. Always prattling on about her feelings and how women should be independent and never *settle*. Just listening to her idiotic opinions made the dermatitis on my ass crack *flare* up. She said there was no way she'd ever leave her school, career, or ambitions for any man. But you know what, Azriel?"

"What?"

"I had her home in my bed that *same* night. She offered herself willingly and pledged her life to me. All within 12 *hours* of meeting me."

Azriel laughed.

It hurt his side and gut to laugh, but he couldn't help it.

"No joke. She belonged to me that very night. Body, mind, and soul."

"Okay. Hell... we have time to kill," said Azriel "I'll play along. How'd you pull that off."

"Don't mock me, Predator. This is serious. To answer your question I simply offered her what she wanted. What *all* beautiful women want. And then I showed her how to get it. Which could only be got through me."

"Oh I gotta hear this," said Azriel. "And what would that be?"

"Immortality. To slowly age, never die. Near eternal beauty."

"How the hell does that do *me* any good?"

"I swear, you guys are such pussies these days. Listen, you're missing the point. I've been alive for a *long* time. I watched entire civilizations rise and fall. I saw the continents move and the oceans shake, the mountains shift. And the one thing that's always been the same is men – kings, rulers, and emperors, and even *monsters*... even the blood-thirsty *tarasque*-destroying themselves because of a woman. Usually not even a very *attractive* woman! I've spent over five millennia studying women. Understanding them. Learning what makes them *tick*. Give me 20 minutes with a happily married woman and I will make her my *concubine* that same night. I'll have her leave her husband. Sacrifice her children to strange gods. Pledge her soul to me. There would be no duress. No trickery. She'd willingly belong to me. I've done it before, my friend."

Azriel laughed again.

This naked vampire with the ridiculous unevenly shaved facial scruff was amusing him. And, if nothing else, the conversation was taking his mind off the pain.

"You keep laughing, you little faggot," said Fezziwig. "How about a demonstration? I will diagnose what happened to you and where you went wrong with your concubine."

"All right."

"And if I am right, and I *will* be, how about a deal?"

"What kind of deal?"

"If I am right and you admit my solution is correct, you will owe me a favor. Any favor I ask now or in the future. If I am wrong, or you find my advice nonsense, I will do you a favor. Any favor you choose – now or in the future. I think it'd be useful to have a Predator owe me a solid. And you would surely find some use for a vampire. Agreed?"

Azriel thought about it.

Yes, he could find having a vampire in his debt useful. And what did he really have to lose? Chances are they'd both be dead soon, anyway.

"All right. I'm in."

"Good. Tell me if I'm wrong. But I'm not, I've heard stories like yours thousands of times," said Fezziwig. "When you first met your concubine she was infatuated with you. You could do no wrong. She *worshipped* the ground you walked on. You had a bad attitude and nasty disposition. You often ignored her in favor of your own pursuits... liked her a little less than she liked you... and she loved it. Other than the occasional female bullshit and feminist nonsense, she was obedient and pleasant and agreeable. Yes?"

"Pretty much."

"Then she started to try to change *you*. She started asking you to not be such a dick to her. To give her more of your time and attention. To prove your love and always get you to say it, *verbally*."

Azriel nodded. It was true. That was exactly what Mina did.

"Then, when you gave her these things, she became... *disagreeable*. Bitchy. Irritated with everything you did – even when you did *nice* things for her. And it all happened after you gave her what she *said* she wanted. Am I right, or do I exaggerate?"

"Not just her. All these girls I get with behave at first and then turn into complete asses," said Azriel.

Fezziwig continued: "They then became disrespectful after you invested money and time trying to get them to be how they were originally when you first met. Yes?"

"Yeah."

"Then eventually they grew bored of you and just wanted to be *friends* – leaving you for a guy who is what you were when they originally fell for you."

Azriel was starting to realize these vampires loved the sound of their own voices. They loved *lecturing*. Rood seemed like he would be the same way, judging by how he behaved, too. Maybe Azriel could use their love of talking to his advantage when they fought Rood again.

"Ready for my advice? And remember, if you don't find it useful, if you laugh at it, if you think it's bullshit... I owe you a favor. But if you know it's true, if you can use it, then you will owe me a favor. A gentleman's bargain. Agreed?"

"All right."

"If you put a concubine on a pedestal she can only look down on you. She doesn't want it no matter how much her rationalization hamster tells her otherwise. But this is exactly what *you* did. And that, my friend, is why you looked like a little faggot to her and she turned on you."

Azriel thought back to the previous night's date. Even before dinner, when she took a break from texting her friends, Mina nagged and complained and criticized: *Omigod, you should be* eating *better. Omigod you are sooooo irritating! Omigod you're like,* manic. *Bipolar. Like calm down. You got* anger *issues. Stop being so needy...*

Fezziwig continued: "You're no different than the many once-great kings I've seen go to war and lose — every record of their existence erased, their people raped and murdered, their books burned — just to impress a woman. Just because they put their women on *pedestals*. It's gotten even worse over the past century. It's why I've begun to think almost all men have become closet *faggots*. She probably nagged you until you wanted to stab her, didn't she?"

"Her and her *phone*," said Azriel,

"I never allow my concubines to possess a phone, it's *forbidden*," said Fezziwig. "But that was her way of telling you to stop being such a little bitch. It wasn't even her fault — it was yours. You didn't make her *your* concubine, she made you *hers*. You rewarded her bad behavior. When she acted unreasonable and stupid, you did something *nice* for her trying to appease her, didn't you?"

"What do you mean?"

"When she nagged and complained, you *bought* her something. When she removed her affection, you gave her more of your time and attention. Yes?"

"Shit. Yeah…"

"I've had hundreds of concubines, Azriel. *Hundreds*. They all think they're little princesses who are more desired than they really are because so many weaklings give them so much attention. They all think they deserve the 'best' guy without having to prove themselves worthy of having the best. They all think they can do *better* the moment you show interest. They all think they want you to change. But they don't. This is why so many men get bitched up. But you know what?"

"Go ahead."

"It's also why women are so easily *manipulated*. "

"Really…"

"It took me hundreds of years to learn what I'm about to tell you," said Fezziwig. "What you do is…"

A flapping noise came from above. Fezziwig stopped talking as a large bat swooped down and landed on the floor in front of them. It turned into the form of a tall, naked, beautiful woman. It was Mara laughing so hard tears were in her eyes. No wonder Azriel's internal radar was sounding off. She'd been there the whole time, listening.

They realized Mara must have snuck in when Azriel was taking his time closing the door overhead. The pain and discussion must have clouded both their senses. Or maybe they were just too tired to care?

Stupid, thought Fezziwig to himself, *stupid old vampire faggot – you just got "got" by a concubine…!*

Neither of them was in good enough shape to fight still. And if Rood came they'd be trapped.

"You boys have a lot to learn about women," laughed Mara. Her breasts shook as she giggled. She held her hands up and her nails grew long and sharp. Her fangs stretched down to her chin. But neither Azriel nor Fezziwig noticed. They were too distracted by her breasts.

"You boys want me to make you a *sammich*," she said clicking her teeth together.

Azriel and Fezziwig stood up, groaning. It hurt just getting to their feet.

The concrete door above started to open again, slow and loud. Azriel and Fezziwig looked at each other. Rood. It had to be him. And now, any hope of survival was gone. They might be able to fight his concubine. But Rood, too? No way. They'd be trapped down there with nowhere to run.

Azriel briefly thought of how much it sucked he'd never be able to apply Fezziwig's advice or get to hear the rest of what he was going to say.

Balls.

Where was this guy a year ago?

And why did he bother telling me – a dude he just met – all this stuff?

Strange…

"The Master is coming down here to join us. Goodie!" Mara laughed as they waited for him to climb down the ladder. They watched the dark figure descend. When it finally reached the ground and it stood behind Mara, both Fezziwig and Azriel had a different reaction and look in their eyes than Mara was expecting.

It wasn't fear or despair. It was *surprise*. Mara turned to greet her master.

But it wasn't her master that greeted her back. It was a long machete that raced towards her neck. Her head fell to the ground, looking up at her attacker with just as much surprise as Azriel and Fezziwig had.

"Son of a bitch…," said Azriel.

"That's right, boy, it's *me*," said the dark figure. "Your bestie!"

It wasn't Rood who opened the door.

It was Finius flashing them his used car salesman smile.

9
ODD BEDFELLOWS

"I want to help you help me help ourselves."

- Crowley
Supernatural

- 1 -

"You're lucky I was able to sniff you out and track you down," said Finius. "Bad enough you let yourself get so *fat* Azzy-boy. But I never thought I'd see you working with a filthy vampire. And a *naked* one at that."

"I know what you are, Zombie. I can *smell* it on you," said Fezziwig.

Fezziwig had killed people for calling him less insulting names than "filthy." But he was too damn old and still in too much pain to fight yet.

Dawn was approaching and all Fezziwig could think about was how much he would like to take a nap. He also had to piss. But there was nowhere to go except on the floor, and his fear of peeing in front of other people made it almost impossible to go with the other two present. The only way he could piss was to go outside and risk being found by Rood. Of course, nothing more than a few drops would probably come out anyway.

"Are you here to get even," said Azriel. "Because it's not going to go well for you if you try…" Azriel didn't really want to fight. His body was still healing and in pain. But he'd have no problem grabbing onto Finius's mind and making him eat himself again if need be.

"How cute. Little Azriel making threats. You can barely stand. But don't worry. Just because you fed me to a zombie and buried me in quicksand for the last year doesn't mean I want to *kill* you. On the contrary. I'm here to *help* you. That is, if you're smart enough to accept. Both our existences are at stake. Truce?"

"For now. How did you escape," said Azriel.

"You *would* like to know, wouldn't you? I'll keep that little diddy to myself." Finius poked Azriel's belly. "Might I suggest Paleo?"

"Quit screwing around, Finius. I have no problem seizing your teeny tiny little mind and tossing you back into the pit again."

"You should know better than to underestimate me by now."

Azriel balled up his fists and felt for that mysterious switch in his mind he used to control Finius last time. He never liked Finius. And he sure as hell didn't trust him. But in this case, he might need him, and didn't want to do anything permanent to him. Not yet, at least. It was tough to resist. Just seeing Finius – the man responsible for the zombie fiasco in the first place, and for his mom, friends, and the entire town being killed – made him want to use the bastard's head as a soccer ball.

"Same temper, eh?" said Finius. "That's good. We'll *need* it. We three have a common enemy. I suggest we put our differences aside. Join forces for mutual… *benefit*…" Finius started looking at Fezziwig like a scientist studying a new specimen.

Fezziwig knew of Finius.

A lot of other monsters knew of him, too.

Many monsters had even gone out of their way to avoid Finius. There were rumors he had been capturing monsters for years, and doing gruesome experiments on them. Fezziwig decided he would keep a close eye on this Finius faggot. The LORD was already telling him via the audible voice inside his head the time was almost ripe to complete his two missions.

Do not hurt Lucifer's favorite, The LORD's voice said. *You need his help.*

The LORD said nothing of Finius, though.

The sly man standing before them was a wild card.

- 2 -

"First things first, gents," said Finius picking up Mara's head. Her eyes were open and blinking, and her mouth was gaping like a fish out of water "We need to dispose of the *trash*. Anyone got a match?"

Azriel and Fezziwig said nothing. The former kept rubbing his still-healing navel where Mara sliced him open. The latter naked, his old body bruised from head to toe, simply stood there.

"Not exactly a couple boy scouts are you? Don't worry. I think I have one," said Finius patting his shirt pockets. He pulled out a long stick from his back pocket. It was about the length of a ruler, and sharp. It looked like it was ripped off a tree branch. He plunged it straight into Mara's heart. Blood spouted out all over her naked body and the floor. Finius reached into his pocket and pulled out a garlic clove. "You guys have no idea how hard it was to find this on such short notice. Luckily *Renfield's Corner Market* still had some. It's old and rotten but should work."

Finius stuffed the clove in the head's mouth.

Then, putting the head on top of the body, he lit a match he found in his shirt pocket, and set the entire body and head on fire. The three watched the bluish-colored flames eat away at the corpse. The fire consumed the flesh until there was nothing but bones and a grinning, fanged skeleton. Smoke filled the room. Fezziwig flipped another switch on the wall and a loud fan behind a vent kicked on. The smoke drifted towards it.

"Rood and his concubine should not be alive," said Fezziwig. "I killed them myself."

"Just another reason you two chuckle heads need me," said Finius with his sleazy smile. Azriel remembered that smile. He also remembered wanting to slap the grin right off Finius's face. "When I escaped my *prison*," continued Finius, cocking an eye at Azriel, "I was weak… my head had just reattached itself to my bodily remains… and it took a while to regenerate. I couldn't even feel my arms and legs for days. It was quite… painful."

"Nobody cares if you hurt. Get to the point." Said Fezziwig. "I don't have long until dawn."

"You're even worse than ASS-riel," said Finius. "Okay, well, the too-long-didn't-read version is, I climbed out of the pit and wandered the town. It didn't take long until I saw Rood and his lovely concubine here feeding on some drifter. They did unspeakable things to the poor fool, too. I'd never seen anything like it. They skinned him alive, right on the street, while having sex with each other. I had to know what was going on around here. I followed them to the basement of the old police station. It used to be a gun range, but now it's a *torture* chamber. There were three other Predators there and I recognized them all. Including your grandma, Azriel."

"*Was* my grandma."

"Was?"

"I killed her. She betrayed me. Joined Rood."

"Pity. I should have known she'd stay on Rood's side. But we really could have *used* her in this fight."

"What do you mean 'stay' on Rood's side?"

"She always was a crazy old hag, Azriel. They sliced and diced them in ways that grossed even *me* out. They cut off her eyelids, and then forced her to *eat* them. I watched from the shadows. They didn't detect me. Their senses were focused on their victims. Two of the predators died and I decided to get out in case they spotted me. They let your grandma go. Told her if she led their vampire cronies to you, they'd reward her. They said they would try to find a way to turn even *your* kind – Predators – into vampires, making her immortal, young, *whole* again. It figured she'd buy into it. That horny old slut was getting senile, would have no problem betraying her own kin. She'd done it before, you know. Azriel your family tree is *full* of treachery. It's practically in your blood."

And I'll start with you, "ally", thought Azriel. I'll stuff you back so deep underground you'll be more likely to be discovered by a Chinaman *than anyone in this town.*

"Bottom line this," said Fezziwig, trying to stifle a yawn and ignoring the growing pressure in his bladder. He could sense the approaching sunrise and was getting sleepy.

"Well, I did hear something. The quicksand pit has a *crack* in it. There is something underneath. Something it's all draining in to. They couldn't enter the quicksand, because it *burns* them. Now that the quicksand is gone they are planning to somehow raise all the dead vampires you buried there. I have no idea how they will do it. I will say this, though, boys… Rood is not an ordinary vampire. He's much, much more."

"No kidding," said Azriel remembering the beating Rood gave him.

"You don't understand. He doesn't have a vampire's vulnerabilities."

"What do you mean?" asked Fezziwig, sitting up.

"I saw him in *sunlight*. Now you tell me, what kind of vampire can do that?" asked Finius. There was a gleam in his eye and he was rubbing his hands together like a comic book super villain. He looked more fascinated with the idea of Rood withstanding sunlight than worried about it.

- 3 -

"That's impossible," said Fezziwig.

No vampire had ever been able to survive sunlight. He fought Rood twice. He knew what Rood was capable of. He had seen his power and strength and fortitude.

But survive sunlight? No. Impossible.

Or was it?

Fezziwig was old enough, and had seen enough, to know nothing was impossible. The fact he was allowed to survive the great flood – which was sent for the specific purpose of killing nephilims like him – was proof of that.

"I beg to differ, Anghel."

"Call me Fezziwig."

Finius stifled a laugh. "All right, *'Fezziwig'*."

"You keep mocking me and I'll cut your tongue out, Zombie," said Fezziwig. "We might need you in this fight. But we don't need your ability to *speak*."

"Enough with the pissing match, boys," said Azriel. "Tell us about this raising up of vampires Rood has planned. Any theories on how he is planning to do it, and how can we stop it?"

"I don't know," said Finius. "I really don't know. How many vampires are in there… *'Fezziwig'*?"

"Hundreds," said Fezziwig standing up, he had his knees bent in towards each other, looking like someone waiting to use the bathroom. "Rood was the first. He and his concubine on the floor here." Fezziwig pointed his six-fingered hand at Mara's smoldering corpse. "After that I scoured the earth looking for the rest of the vampires. I wanted to *purge* the earth of them. I never should have created any of them. When I discovered this town, the quicksand pit, I had the pit *blessed* – turning the water in the quicksand holy. Holy water is like acid to us. It's worse than sunlight. Even if they somehow survived they should have been floating in agonizing *pain*. But now they are walking around in broad daylight. My apologies, I can't take it anymore. I have to piss…"

Fezziwig walked to the corner. To hell with his stage fright or the fact there was no drain or anywhere for the urine to go. He held his flaccid penis and stood there shuffling his feet, coughing and waiting.

Nothing came out.

"Come ON!" he said looking at his penis. "Piss dammit! PISS!"

"Prostate?" said Finius.

"I will need blood soon, too," said Fezziwig ignoring Finius's question.

"How long has it been since you fed," said Azriel.

"Too long."

"How long can you go until you need to feed."

"No more than a few days. Blood to me is like *water* to you. It's the elixir of life for my kind. No matter how much food I eat, I still need fresh blood, like you need water. If I don't get it often, I die."

"So what's the plan then," said Azriel looking at Finius. He figured Finius was cooking up some kind of scheme. And, knowing him, it probably involved betraying one or both of him and Fezziwig.

"We do what people have always done when a vampire came to town," said Finius. He kicked the bones around in the dying fire. "We storm the castle with torches and pitchforks."

- 4 -

Finius's plan was simple:

As far as they knew, only Rood was able to withstand sunlight. He didn't think Mara or the other vampires could. At least, he hadn't seen them in sunlight. So for now he assumed Rood's other vampires would be incapacitated in the daylight, making that the perfect time to strike Rood's lair. They would go in hard and fast and not even bother sneaking around. It would have to be just Finius and Azriel. Fezziwig couldn't be in the daylight and it was already dawn. It would have been ideal for him to come. But he was already curled up in the corner, sound asleep before they even left.

They could run, of course.

It would be easy enough to leave town.

But that wouldn't stop Rood from raising hundreds of vampires and finding them later. None of them wanted to live on a planet run over with vampires led by something as evil and powerful as Rood.

He had already been turning people into vampires. But as Fezziwig told them before drifting off to sleep:

"Those are third generation vampires. I call them *tier 3 vampires*. Those are vampires spawned from the vampires I personally turned. Each generation gets a bit weaker – like a copy of a copy. It's not unlike how the zombies are, which shouldn't be too surprising considering me and the head zombie both had the same *father*. Tier 3's are only a little stronger than humans. They have no control of their abilities, and even those are weak. They are like young fish that need guidance to swim and survive in the same stream. Most don't live long on their own. And they have always been easy pickings for Predators and other monsters and even humans who discovered them. The vampires I hunted and tossed in the quicksand are far more powerful. I turned them myself. I trained them how to survive, how to fight, how to *hunt*. They are stronger, more deadly. They are like Rood in as much as they know what they're capable of and how to control their abilities. They can withstand all kinds of attacks. If Rood is able to get them to somehow *obey* him... I certainly never could get them to obey me... and if they are somehow immune to sunlight, too, they'd be unstoppable. None of us would survive long. There aren't enough Predators to stop it. Even the other monsters would be forced to join Rood or die."

Finius and Azriel armed themselves with as many stakes as they could.

But would they even work on Rood?

Granny said she plunged a stake into Rood's heart and he laughed. But she was a liar and a traitor and couldn't be trusted. They knew something was making Rood powerful. Something allowed him to become far more dangerous than Fezziwig or any other vampire.

What was it?

None of them knew.

But they knew they were going to find out.

And, probably, the hard way.

- 5 -

"Listen Azriel," said Finius, as they walked down Main Street away from the town square fountain. Azriel was distracted by the empty building that used to belong to his dentist Dr. Barlow. The sign still said: *Dr. Barlow: Telling you the "tooth" every time!* He had a memory of his mother Irma walking him in there as a child before his blue pill days. Azriel had a cavity being filled in and he remembered suppressing the urge to take the drill out of Dr. Barlow's hand, and plunging it into his eyeball.

"What," said Azriel, annoyed at Finius interrupting his memory. Good memories were in short supply these days. And he relished them when they happened.

"I know you don't trust me. And God knows I don't trust you. But neither of us should be trusting this vampire. We should destroy him now, while he's asleep. You know your instincts want to kill him."

"My instincts want me to kill you."

"I'm serious, boy."

"I'm pretty serious, too."

"We need to kill him. He's dangerous."

"Fezziwig is off limits to you. He saved my life and I owe him. He's probably the closest thing I have to a *friend* in this screwy world," said Azriel thinking about how useful the old vampire's advice about women was. Azriel technically owed Fezziwig a favor, too, since Fezziwig won their bet. "You touch him and I kill you. Period. This isn't a discussion. I will mind fuck you again, make you eat yourself. Understood?"

"Suit yourself, boy. Don't say I didn't *warn* you. Monsters are never to be trusted. You should know this better than most."

Azriel was almost healed from his earlier wounds and the cuts were mostly just faint scars now. They approached the police station from the parking lot that, at one time, Azriel, Finius, and Pastor Shane had scoped the zombie cops out from.

Seeing the station unchanged – with the big hole still in the front door from when Finius's truck went through it – brought back all the horrible memories Azriel spent the last few years forgetting about. Especially the one of a giant Chief Rawger chaining Azriel to the jail and coming back with live people, eating them in front of his eyes, biting into their skulls like he was eating an *apple*... swallowing people whole, chewing their brains, and talking with his mouth full of flesh and brain and bone, spraying it while he talked, meat flying out of his filed-sharp teeth.

It was more horror than his mind could tolerate.

It took *years* to fight through it.

Yet, here he was again.

He was about to go back into the same station, with Finius of all people, and have another show down, drag-out battle with something spawned from the same evil angel DNA that created the monsters in the first place. Something Azriel would have to kill, or be killed by, yet again.

Same story and stage, different monsters. This is almost too deja vu, he thought yet again, as they approached the door.

- 6 -

"You ready, Azriel? I'm not the pessimist type. But we're probably not going to live through this," said Finius holding a stake in each hand. Although "stake" wasn't the most accurate word. They were just sticks and sharpened pieces of lumber. The machete Finius used to decapitate Mara was secured to his side via his belt.

"Let's get this over with," said Azriel.

He was not so much scared as he was excited.

Even anxious.

Yes, he probably would die.

But he *wanted* this fight.

"Okay then. The plan is we run in and attack anything that moves. Since Rood's third tier vampires will be asleep it will just be him," said Finius.

- 7 -

Finius and Azriel entered the artificially widened police station door. They made straight for the door to the basement. The hallway was dark and had been cleared out by whoever cleaned out the skeletons and remains left over from when Chief Rawger ruled that particular kingdom.

Azriel wondered how the authorities explained it all away.

There wasn't even a single news story about it.

Granny said the government probably had something to do with that.

If so, how many other atrocities did the government keep quiet about? How many other monster related murders, genocides, and blood baths did Uncle Sam sweep under the rug and dispatch bounty hunter Predators to clean up?

It was an interesting thought. A thought Azriel would put more time into investigating later. Assuming there *was* a later.

They made it to the basement stairway door. Azriel ripped it off the hinges. Finius stared at him with what looked like a cross between awe and curiosity. Azriel looked at him back, his eyes glowing red, and held on to the door. They nodded at each other and went down into the basement gun range-turned-torture-chamber.

They expected it to be dark. But they could see a light down the stairs – sunlight, from the look of it – illuminating the space. Maybe Rood was home? Surely he knew they were there. And this time Azriel would be ready for him. Or so he thought.

As they reached the bottom of the stairs they were met not just with Rood – but over two dozen vampires, all wide awake, and none of them burning from the sunlight pouring in through the small windows along the ceiling. The vampires hissed and surrounded them.

Azriel and Finius heard clapping and a loud "TOOT! TOOT! TOOT!" from Rood's corncob pipe coming from the doorway behind them.

"You're just in time, boys," said Rood.

Azriel's body was tensed and pulsating with adrenaline and power – ready to strike. Finius looked less angry, and more shocked, as if thinking, *"Where the hell did all these vampires come from? How are they not melting in the sunlight? I hadn't calculated this... oh shit..."*

"Time for what," said Azriel, a stake in each hand gripped so tightly his knuckles were white.

"Why, my vampire *apocalypse*, of course."

10
SKIPPER OF SKIN

"It's a swell ship for the skipper, but a hell ship for the crew."

- Author Unknown

- 1 -

"Quit being such a baby," said Rood, tooting his pipe. "You Predators are remarkably like little girls when it comes to a bit of *pain*." When Rood said "pain," he sliced into Azriel's navel – which had just healed less than an hour earlier – with a rusty straight razor that looked like Mara's. Rood was beginning the process of skinning Azriel alive and was frustrated without Mara's guidance.

The "fight" between Rood's vampires and Azriel and Finius ended quickly.

Azriel and Finius managed to stake or behead all but two of the tier 3 vampires before Rood easily overpowered, disarmed, and bound them. He then stripped Azriel and Finius naked, and set them upon metal tables. Their hands, arms, legs, and feet were bound with thick chains, tied in such a way where the more they moved, the more the chains around their necks choked them.

It was extremely painful.

And, for Azriel, humiliating.

What a way to die – naked, at the hands of a sadistic vampire with a captain's hat on his head, blowing on a corncob pipe.

Rood sliced into Azriel's flesh again and eyed the cut with disappointment. It was like he knew he was doing it wrong.

"You two see that sign?" said Rood, pointing with his pipe to a plaque on the wall. "It says 'This is a swell ship for the skipper, but a hell ship for the crew.' I find it *so* accurate, don't you? I've been collecting these sea-themed signs lately. I have one in the bathroom that says 'Poop Deck' and another in my crypt that says 'All who enter must surrender the booty'."

Rood tooted his pipe, followed by several shorter toots as he laughed.

"That's quite a *fat* stomach, Azriel. I know it sounds strange, but it makes skinning you more complicated. I'm used to thinner victims like people of the *cloth*. In my day I used to travel from church to church seizing and torturing priests and nuns and deacons and choir ladies and boys. None of them were fat. Then again, it's been a few hundred years. And from what

117

I've seen so far, almost everyone is fat nowadays. Hmm."

Rood stared at Azriel's belly like it was a puzzle.

He continued, "You healed nicely though already from Mara's razor. I wonder how long I can skin you before it grows *back*? Oh, this is going to be FUN!"

Rood tooted his pipe again.

His captain's hat cast a shadow over his glowing red eyes.

"Unfortunately, since you killed my concubine I'm flying blind here. She's so much better at skinning people than I am. I'm rather messy and crude. It probably *hurts* more when I do it, though. But I lack her artistic touch, I'm afraid. My projects bleed out too quickly. Where are her remains, gentlemen? I don't expect you to tell me. Probably hiding with Fezziwig while he sleeps in his 'secret' chamber?"

Rood did air quotes when he said "secret."

"You should have seen Mara's delicate precision when she sliced off the old woman's eyelids and carved into her sagging tits, Azriel. The old hag's screams were like *music*. And the way she threatened to *rape* me for daring to mutilate her was the kind of entertainment you can't pay for!"

Another toot on his pipe.

Rood was still distracted by his last cut on Azriel's stomach, as if he was staring at a chessboard, concentrating on his next move.

"But she should have been grateful. After all, her eyeballs were left untouched, I didn't *blind* her, at least."

Rood made another incision in Azriel's chest. Azriel grimaced from the pain, but refused to make a sound. He wasn't going to give Rood the satisfaction of yelling out, no matter what he did. It seemed like Rood was trying to diagram how he was going to skin Azriel, and was screwing it up. As far as Azriel was concerned, if Rood was going to skin him alive at least this bastard could do it *right*.

"By the way, does my pipe bother you?" said Rood taking a step back from the table. He took his captain's hat off and slicked his hair back. "I originally found it annoying myself. But it's *grown* on me. I got it from the man who saved me from the pit. Can you believe that? I feel I owe him some kind of *homage*. It was pure blind luck he found me. He said he was traveling with his family through town and they stopped to see the pits. I guess the fact nobody lived in town didn't bother him as he barreled downtown pulling a lovely sailboat. His wife and daughter were in the car with him. The boat is a beauty. Can't wait to *sail* it now that I can withstand sunlight. Surely you saw it? I used it to block the freeway entrance.

"Anyway, where was I? My apologies for getting off-track. I seem to have a shorter attention span than I used to have. Ah, yes, the family. When they saw the sack my remains were in, sitting in the draining quicksand pit, they must have pulled it to the banks and opened it. I'm not sure how it happened... my resurrection, I mean. But there is a power in those pits that *likes* me. I resurrected right in front of them! You should have seen the looks in their eyes! It was priceless! When they saw me, naked, hungry, jittery from lack of sustenance – the man wearing this hat sucking on this pipe must have taken pity on me. The fool. He should have feared me. I cannot believe how *naive* people are. I drained him, his wife, and his daughter of every drop of blood in their bodies. I was starving. Oh how *good* it tasted! It felt like I hadn't fed in centuries. Hey, do you want to know a secret?"

Azriel stared at the vampire. Sweat rolled off his brow. This long-winded thing that wouldn't shut up was carving him up and it hurt like nothing he'd ever experienced before. He couldn't help but remember Granny talking about how she saw Rood skin one of the Predator's *dicks*.

Rood put his mouth next to Azriel's ear. His breath smelled like a dead skunk. He whispered: "I love hearing and watching people suffer. I simply *thrive* on it. The more someone screams and yells and cries, the better their blood tastes."

Rood stood up straight again.

"And that family... they were *screamers*. This hat and this pipe just looked like so much... fun, how could I resist taking them? The man had it rigged with this whistle in it so it toots like a foghorn. How creative!

"Anyway, when people started coming into the town, passing in and by, mostly drifters and the occasional person stopping by for supplies, I would simply capture them and feed. Some of them I turned, like the ones you just killed. No matter. I will create *more* later tonight. Far more powerful ones, too. By the way, do you know what I tell my new vampires after I create them, Azriel? Try to guess."

Azriel looked at Rood refusing to show how much pain he was in. He could hardly think straight, much less speak. But he wasn't going to give this thing the satisfaction. It admitted it fed on misery. And he wasn't going to *nourish* it.

"I tell them to call me 'The Skipper' – ha! Ha! Not Rood. Not Master. Just Skipper. In fact this is funny. When one of them forgot to call me Skipper I decided to make an *example* of him. I had him staked, beheaded, and burned. I have a lot more control over them than I thought I would. They are very obedient to me. But you know how it is. You have to treat your new vampires like you treat new *concubines*. No matter how obedient they are, you have to make them show some *respect*. Otherwise, it's nothing but chaos and anarchy and back talk and drama like you wouldn't believe! And when that happens I have to *waste* time and go and kill them and it's all just such a drag, you know?"

Rood plunged his razor into Azriel's leg when he said "waste." Blood shot out from the wound. Azriel still refused to make a sound.

"For fuck's sake you vampires *talk* too much," said Azriel. His voice sounded shaky and strained. "If you're going to kill me just... *do* it already."

Rood laughed. It was a deep, dark laugh. Evil. There was no pipe toot, though, the pipe was in his hand.

"I know what you're trying to do, my young friend. It won't work. You're trying to get me angry... maybe even *stall* me. Yes? You think you will conjure up a way to escape? Sorry, it won't work. But here's good news. I am not going to kill you. Not yet, at least. I have use for you first. Well, not you, but something you *possess*. You see, first I'm going to skin you alive like I did the other Predators I caught. They were screamers before they died, you know. Oh they tried to be defiant like you are. They played the tough guy role. They threatened to kill me. But I just kept skinning and slicing them. It's like the ultimate chess game. How long will it take to make a Predator scream? And you *will* scream, Azriel. I promise you that. Then you know what I'm going to do? I'm going to drink all your blood. Every last drop. It'll taste horrible – but maybe less horrible after you scream? We shall see. All you Predators taste horrible to me. I vomited the first few times I tried to drink Predator blood. When I drank the last two Predators who came here you want to know what they said? It concerns you, Azriel."

"What..." said Azriel, trying to sound like he wasn't straining from the pain.

"Your own kind fears you Azriel, did you know that? They said you have especially powerful energies stored inside you. And, what can I say, I *needed* to see for myself. That's why I made that deal with your grandma to lead my boys to you, bring you back dead or alive – as long as you didn't *bleed* out. I told her I'd let her live when it came time to raise the rest of my brothers whom old Fezziwig killed.

"I have to admit though, I half expected her to turn on me when she brought you back. Kind of *hoped* she would. I guess she figured my team was the winner even though she probably couldn't be turned, anyway. And you know what, Azriel? She was right, wasn't she? Pity she let herself get killed. I was starting to like the horny old ding bat."

"So that really is the plan, then," said Finius. "Raise the dead vampires in the pit...?" Finius was, as Rood incessantly talked on, purposely not bringing attention to himself. Azriel figured it was to save his own skin for as long as possible. But knowing Finius, he had an escape plan figured out. If he could escape his safe, then maybe he could get out of these chains.

Rood turned around to address Finius's table and wiped his rusty straight razor on his smock. Azriel noticed Rood had Finius's machete clipped to his belt behind him. "Would you like to hear my plans? I don't mind telling you boys. There's no possibility you can stop me anyway. Would you like to hear it?"

Rood tooted his pipe again, turned back to Azriel, and cut into a patch of skin on Azriel's belly. It made a ripping noise as he peeled off a small strip of skin. Azriel stifled his desire to yell. He didn't know how much longer he could hold out, though. This shit *hurt*.

- 2 -

"To be honest I am not sure how I was resurrected or how I'm even alive. As I said, someone powerful around here must *like* me. I sense a lot of evil in this town. It feels good! I think it's what drew me here in the first place. Back then this wasn't a town, you know. There was just an empty church out here in the forest. I never did figure out who built it. I remember finding it and being disappointed there were no priests or holy men to skin and torture. What a waste! But then your friend Fezziwig killed me good and proper. Do you know what he did to me? Did he tell you? He turned into a bat and flew into my mouth and down my throat and into my stomach and then… BAM….!"

Rood plunged the razor into Azriel's shoulder so deep it hit bone. Azriel couldn't fight back a small gasp. He wished he at least had something to *bite* down on.

Rood continued: "Fezziwig turned back into his normal vampire form. Inside my stomach. It was brilliant! *Painful*… but brilliant! I really have to hand it to the old blood-gobbler," said Rood, followed by a toot on his pipe. "But hundreds of years later I was *plucked* out of the pit like this razor."

Rood pulled out the razor stuck in Azriel's shoulder as he said "plucked." The blood trickled towards the hilt. Drops pitter-pattered to the floor. Rood smelled the blood-soaked razor. His made a face of disgust. He then wheeled an IV machine over to Azriel's table. The IV machine was attached to a catheter and needle. Rood jabbed the needle in Azriel's neck. He missed the jugular on purpose.

"Whoops?"

He tried again. This time he connected with Azriel's jugular. The blood started coming. But it moved unusually slow. Rood smelled Azriel's neck again.

"*Yecht!* Your blood even *smells* disgusting," he said. "You know, I wasn't joshing you… I really did throw up the first few times I tried drinking a Predator's blood. I found this out a few weeks after I was rescued from the pit. The quicksand pit was deeper then. Not sure what's happening to it or making it drain. But even then I could sense all my vampire brothers – all of Fezziwig's spawns – buried in there. Dead. Nothing but charred skulls and bone ashes. When my naked foot accidentally touched the sand, it burned! That sly old vampire had the pit *blessed*. Very painful. Also very brilliant. I almost don't want to kill him. What other secrets could he teach me?

"Anyway, there goes that low-attention span again! Does everyone in this era have that problem? Where was I? Oh yes... the night I was miraculously resurrected, I was naked and replenished from feeding on the boat guy's family. I didn't know what year it was or how long I had been dead. But it was around midnight judging by the moon. People would arrive on some days, and look at those quicksand pits, like it was some kind of tourist attraction. I fed like a king. But I knew I'd need *assistants*. I had never even seen a truck or automobile before then. My new vampire spawns filled me on what had happened in the past few hundred years. Fascinating. I still cannot believe how *fat* most of you people have gotten. Back when I was human I had a fat wife. She was the only fat person I knew within 100 miles. Now it looks like you have to travel 100 miles to find someone who *isn't* fat. How things have changed!"

Rood carved another line in Azriel's belly, and up towards his chest. He was apparently trying to draw something on Azriel's stomach. "Come now, Azriel, I *know* this hurts. It's okay to tell me it hurts. It's okay to cry, little Predator."

Azriel glared at him. He'd endure for as long as he could. He saw Finius from the corner of his eye moving ever so slowly.

What was that *slippery* bastard up to?

- 3 -

"Within weeks I'd turned dozens more people into vampires. Whenever someone would stop in town I would spy on them as a bat at night as they talked about Belasco being *haunted*. I believe it is haunted, too. I can feel spirits in that pit here – under the surface. Not *ghosts*, mind you. But something else. Something sinister and evil and *hungry*. Kindred souls, if you will. What a delightful town! I instantly loved it here!

"I was going to leave with my new children; we had to feed, after all. But then... something fell into my lap, you could say."

Rood slashed Azriel's belly as he said the word "lap" and tooted his pipe. Azriel was letting his anger and rage build. It helped with the pain, and gave him something else to focus on.

The first thing I'm gonna do when I get free is shove that pipe up his ass.

"I had an encounter with one of your kind Azriel – a Predator. I'd only fought and killed one once, back before Fezziwig killed me. But this particular Predator said he was looking for *you* of all people. Even said your name. He said... let me see if I can remember... 'I'm not here to fight you vampire, I'm here to kill Azrael.' He called you Azrael not Azriel. I remember. Can you believe that? Apparently you have angered even some of your own kind! I don't know if I should hate you or *love* you.

"Of course, I told him thank you for not coming to kill me. You see, I hadn't tasted blood in two days. I was starving. The thirst we vampires have without blood… it was like when I nearly died of dehydration when I got lost in the woods as a boy. But a hundred times *worse*. So what did Yours Truly do? I killed him, of course! It was a brutal, ugly battle. He nearly chopped my body in half with this thing you call a 'chainsaw'! But I won. I killed him by cutting off his head and tossing it right into that quicksand pit."

Rood pointed towards the door in the direction of the quicksand with his pipe.

"I'm… proud of you, Dracula," said Azriel, in a feeble attempt to mock the vampire and refusing to show any pain, which was nearly intolerable.

"You should be more grateful, Azriel, not mock me. He came to kill you, after all. I wonder Azriel, how many others like him are there? How many want to kill you? And why? Even your own grandma betrayed you to save her own skin. Hey, I just made a joke, did you catch it? Save her own 'skin'? ha! Ha!"

Azriel did wonder about that. He'd never even met another Predator before his grandma saved him. But he remembered Pastor Shane saying there were people and *things* looking for him. Unfortunately, Pastor Shane never said why, and Azriel never had time to ask before the old pastor died.

Rood looked at Azriel's stomach, inserted his long fingernails under two spots, and lifted up, ripping a huge swath of skin off. Azriel bit his teeth together as hard as he could, sweat rolled down his face, and he let out a slight grunt.

Rood held the skin up in the light with two hands for Azriel to see. It looked like a half circle with two triangles on top.

"Drats!" said Rood. "It was supposed to be in the shape of a *sailboat*! No matter. When I bring Mara back tonight she will show me how she does it. But first I really want to tell you about this Predator's blood. I want to tell you what it *did* to me. I find it to be the ultimate poetic justice."

Rood kept looking at his work of art, holding it up in the light, as he spoke. He looked disappointed.

Azriel tried to look at Finius through the corner of his eye. He dared not move his neck due to the chains choking him the more he moved. But he knew Finius was up to something.

He'd fought Finius before. He'd seen Finius fight. He'd seen how fast, and agile, and skilled he was. Finius had even somehow escaped his safe. Surely he had some plan to escape his chains? And what if he did? After what Azriel did to him he'd probably get his revenge on Azriel, and not help him.

Or would he?

Finius said his whole reason – twisted as it was – for bringing that zombie head to Belasco was to force Azriel to be what he was born to be. To help him with his *destiny*.

Finius was a complicated man.

Only time would tell what his plan was.

- 4 -

"The blood tasted worse than anything I could imagine. Remember how I just said I was lost in the woods as a boy, and dehydrated? Well, I nearly died of *starvation*, too. I finally found a creek to drink from and saw a dead fish on the banks. It stunk and was rotten. I ate it! Oh it was NASTY! Made me not want to eat *meat* anymore. I threw up while eating it. But I was starving and a starving person will eat just about anything. It probably is why I hated eating meat after that. Ah well. But guess what, boys? When I killed that Predator I was starving. So I drank his blood. I *choked* that blood down! It was awful. Tasted like poison. I blacked out after taking it – the taste was *that* bad. I blacked out for so long, I woke up later in the daylight. The daylight! It had knocked me out for hours. But I found the daylight didn't hurt me anymore! Can you believe that? I was also taller. And *stronger!*"

Rood tooted his pipe again.

His lips formed a tight grin around the handle.

"Azriel you have no idea. Dying from sunlight is very painful." Rood impaled Azriel's arm with the razor as he said "painful."

Blood squirted out of Azriel's arm.

Still no scream.

Rood was growing more and more annoyed at Azriel's lack of showing pain.

"Drats… I have to be careful! I want to *skin* you, not bleed you out! That's what this IV is for. Your blood will be especially powerful to me, I think. Whatever it is that makes your kinds' blood empower me… I have no idea what it is… but you are supposed to be special, Azriel. The Predator I killed said you were *dangerous*, even. That you had a dark destiny and needed to die. Did you know that? I bet you didn't know that. I was actually very surprised by how easily you were defeated. I expected much more of a fight from you."

"Piss… off…" said Azriel.

It was all he could think to say without showing pain.

His hair and face were drenched in sweat.

"Damn you, you're stubborn though. What if I sliced off your eyelids like Mara did your grandma? Or skinned your dick? No… I better not. I'm not skilled enough with this yet. I might actually cut your eyes out or your dick off and you might bleed out too fast. Can't waste even another *drop* of your precious blood. I bet it will taste even *worse* than the others… I'm kind of dreading it actually, if you want to know the truth. But I think yours will give me even more power. I bet there's something damn near magical about *your* blood.

"Do you want to know what else your kind's blood does for me? Do you? You will love this! You see, when I drank the Predator's blood and went back to the basement here where my children were sleeping that day… I found all of them *dead*. They'd died of hunger. No blood for too long killed them. In my battle with the Predator I sustained some serious wounds. I was bleeding a little. Not much. We vampires are fast healers already. But I was healing much faster than usual. And while inspecting my ilk some of my blood dripped onto one of them. He immediately *revived*! His eyes opened and he gasped for breath. It was like he'd never perished. Predator blood made me resistant to sunlight and allowed my blood to resurrect other vampires from the dead! I couldn't believe it! So I naturally woke them all up one by one and headed for the draining quicksand pit. There was something I wanted in those pits. So I went after it."

Azriel heard a "clicking" sound coming from Finius's table. It was faint. And Finius only did it while Rood was talking or tooting his pipe. Finius was up to something. But if Rood heard him, they'd be done for. Plan over.

Azriel decided to keep the bloviating vampire talking.

It obviously liked the sound of its own voice anyway.

"Don't keep me in… suspense," said Azriel fighting the pain. "What was at the pit?"

"Why, my *concubine* Mara of course. She's stunning, isn't she? I've never seen a more proportioned woman in my life. And her eyes… so cold, so *diabolical!* I figured she was probably in there near where I was found. So I had my children go to the main highway and capture someone. It was risky doing that. Didn't want to call attention to ourselves. It was one thing to capture people who stopped by in town. It is quite another to be seen on the main highway doing it. But it was *worth* it. They were able to find someone on the side of the highway with a broken down car and bring her back. She was a mother of three kids. She was also a *Christian* – had a gold cross around her neck and everything. I love Christian blood! It's my favorite. It's like eating *dessert*. And the more faithful and strong their beliefs, the *better* their blood tastes. I couldn't wait to drink her! So we took the kids and told her if she didn't do as we said and fetch the sack I figured Mara's remains were in, we'd kill them. Truth is, although I pride myself on being a vampire of my word… a rather *inconvenient* habit from my Pastor days… we were going to kill her kids anyway. But she didn't know that."

Rood tooted on his pipe and smiled.

Azriel could hear more clicking noise from Finius's table and kept Rood talking.

"Why…" said Azriel. There was a pool of sweat on his table. His skin was paler as the catheter in his neck drained his blood. It drained slowly, like a thick milk shake through a straw.

"Why what?"

"Why bring a woman to the pit."

"Oh yes, well, I was immune to sunlight and so were my children now. Although they were still much weaker than I am. You see there's a hierarchy with vampires. Fezziwig is the strongest. Or was. He's so old now. But even his old body is much stronger than mine would ordinarily be. When I find him, and I will, I'll be killing him as quickly as possible. He's dangerous. Did you see how *fast* he could move? The old man has the moves even at his age."

"Me and my brothers and sisters – those of us turned by Fezziwig directly are a little weaker than him. We aren't quite as fast and strong. But the vampires we turn, well, they are only a little stronger than when they are humans, frankly. But my blood allowed them to at least bare sunlight. It hurts them. Like a sunburn. But they can live in it and walk through it.

"I didn't know if holy water affected me still. It damn near burned my toes off before. So off to the pits we went. I tested the remaining quicksand – not even ankle deep by then – to see if drinking that Predator's blood made me safe from holy water. No such luck. It still burned like *hell*… but I wonder Azriel, after I drain *your* blood – as powerful as you're supposed to be – will I be immune even to holy water? What say you, Azriel? Hmm?"

"So…. what happened," asked Azriel still wanting to distract Rood for as long as possible. It was all he could do to not pass out from the pain. He could feel the skin Rood ripped off slowly growing back.

"Well, I sent the woman into the quicksand to where I could sense where my Mara was. I get aroused just thinking about her and all the wickedness we've done! I sent her down into the quicksand which wasn't even knee-deep, and even gone in some spots. The lady's children's lives were at stake, after all. I told her if she helps me save my child, I'll spare *hers*. So she did it. And by gum she came back up with Mara's skull and a handful of her remains, a few charred bone fragments, mostly. Would it be enough? I didn't know. But I had the woman wipe the sand off the skull and bones. I bled a few drops of my own blood into the skull's mouth and Mara's body started coming back to life! Regenerating from nothing! Predator blood is truly amazing! Her skin and arms and legs started forming. A few minutes later she was *whole* again. She was the beautiful, cold-hearted, generously-breasted concubine I knew of yore! And as a gift I gave her the woman and her children. All for herself. After all, several hundred years sleep works up quite the *appetite*! I'd have preferred giving my concubine someone more *officially holy*, like a priest. But beggars can't be choosers, right?"

Rood tooted his pipe over and over, pleased with himself.
Azriel could no longer hear Finius picking the lock.
Was Finius stumped?
Was it over?

- 5 -

"My Mara was back! And she was *hungry*! And I'd never seen her so ruthlessly and viciously attack before. The kids screamed and Mara made the mom watch her kill and torture them, before draining her. It was a symphony for the eyes! It's also when I got the idea to send vampires out to find *other* Predators. I wanted more Predator blood. I wanted more of the power it gave me. It took a couple months, but we managed to lure a few back here, like your grandma and a couple others. I spent hours torturing them for the whereabouts of other Predators.

"The few we did find and lure back here kept bringing up your name. They kept saying *Azrael* was the one they feared the most. The 'strongest one.' Your Granny told me your name was Azriel and said that name turned her on more. Weird woman her.

"I drank all their blood except your grandma's. She said she knew where you were. She said if I let her go she'd bring you back here. So I sent some of my children with her to back her up and *Ta Daa!* Here you are on my table. Being sliced and diced and ready to be *drank* up. I've almost got two pint bags filled with your blood over here, see?" Rood held up the bags. Azriel struggled to stay conscious.

"And not a minute too soon! I was hoping you'd make it here for my final encore. The quicksand pit is completely gone now. I don't know what's draining it or how. Nor do I care. But it's drained down enough where I can walk in and revive my brothers and sisters. There are hundreds of them down there. And when I revive them, we will feast on your blood. You see Azriel, I'm not going to kill you. I'm going to keep you alive for a very, very long time. Draining your blood to feed us all. I will keep you weak from lack of blood, but not let you die. That will give us power. Power to resist the sunlight. Power to kill and take anything we want – human, Predator, or monster. Even the *demons* wandering the earth right now will have no choice but to follow me.

"Azriel, it'll be a true apocalypse. A *vampire* apocalypse. Won't that be nice?"

Rood tooted on his pipe over and over and started doing a jig dance around the room. "And you want to know what else I noticed, Azriel?" he said, skipping across the room, from one wall to the next.

Azriel stared at him. He would kill this son of a bitch. And he would do it *tonight*. Azriel didn't know how – Rood was so jacked up on power, and he was weakened by blood loss and pain – but he was going to do it, or die trying.

"I'll tell you," said Rood. "It turns out, when I revive these vampires, they *obey* me. I can control their will. They have to obey my commands. And you know what else? I can kind of see why Fezziwig hunted us all down and exterminated us. I really can. We were chaotic. Unruly. Unorganized. We hate authority and do as we please. We called attention to ourselves to indulge in our own self-gratifications. We endangered each other with our recklessness. He had no choice, our urges are too powerful. Not ripping out the throats of the nearest person and draining them of blood is like you dying of thirst each day and refusing to drink water handed to you.

"But that won't be the case with me. No, no, no… you see, my ilk that I resurrect *obey* me. Even Mara doesn't rebel like she used to. She's completely obedient to me. I will lead them, my own private *army*. Imagine what several hundred vampires like me all juiced up on Predator blood, immune to sunlight, and nearly impossible to destroy can accomplish!"

Rood said this as he took the pipe out of his mouth, grabbed one of the blood bags, poked a hole in it with his long, sharp pinky finger nail, and readied to drink from it.

- 6 -

"Here goes nuttin'," said Rood. He closed his eyes and prepared for the horrible taste.

Azriel wasn't surprised his blood disgusted the vampire, just as his taste disgusted the zombies. But Rood was strong. He had an indomitable will. His stomach wretched and heaved as he drank, and blood poured down his chin onto his neck. He kept drinking, stopping every few seconds to hold in his vomit. Eventually, he drained the first bag, but was too disgusted to even look at the second bag, which he set on the floor.

"Holy shit! HOLY SHIT!!!" yelled Rood.

His body tensed and his eyes shifted and glowed bright red. He looked like he was radiating raw power.

"The power… the strength… look at me…" he said. Rood started growing taller. And within moments he was so tall his head nearly hit the ceiling.

Then there was a tap on his shoulder.

He turned around and noticed two things:

First, Finius was now standing on his table. His chains were on the floor. And second, the machete Rood had clipped to his belt was now rushing at his neck, slicing through.

Rood's head fell to the floor and his body followed suit.

"And you say *I* talk too much, Azzy-boy" said Finius, spitting on Rood's body.

- 7 -

As Finius was undoing Azriel's chains, Rood's head was already starting to re-attach to his body. Finius had no garlic to stuff in the head's mouth, no matches to light the body on fire with, no stake to drive through his heart.

And if he did, would it even matter? Probably not for Rood.

Rood was already almost *impossible* to kill. The Predator blood made him nearly invincible. Maybe if they had some holy water… maybe. But they didn't. The only holy water was now taken by whatever strange mechanism was draining the quicksand lake. As Finius undid Azriel's chains he would periodically stop to slash at the veins and tendons re-attaching, slowing the vampire's resurrection.

"Hurry, let's get out of here!" said Finius running up the stairs. "Grab his head, we need to keep it separate from his body!"

Azriel grabbed Rood's head and they ran up the stairs into the main station hallway.

The two vampires that had survived were nowhere to be found. Where were they?

Finius assumed they must be out looking for Fezziwig. It would be night soon – Rood had spent half the day figuring out a way to tie them up in such a way where the more they moved, the more it choked them, then let them sit for a few hours to stew in fear, and then another couple hours torturing them – so if they did find Fezziwig, he'd probably be awake and waiting for them.

Or, so they hoped.

As they reached the top stoop Azriel felt a rush of weakness hit him. He had lost two pints of blood and was dizzy. He tripped over one of the vampires they killed. Rood's head flew out of his hands and rolled back down the stairs into the basement towards the body. Azriel could hear it already starting to re-attach itself.

Balls!

"You idiot!" yelled Finius. "Never mind it, let's go!"

Finius was right.

There was no going back for it.

They ran naked down Main Street to the fountain, and into the trap door. Thunderclouds started rolling in and lighting flashed as if the sky was getting ready to witness an epic battle. Rain started pouring on them. It soothed Azriel's still-healing stomach a little. They climbed down the ladder, Azriel first, Finius next, who closed the door behind them.

"Fezziwig we have trouble, they're all coming back. The vampires – *your* vampires – are about to be *raised*..." said Azriel.

But nobody heard him.

Fezziwig was gone.

11
VAMPIRE APOCALYPSE

"The water is poisoned!"

- Doctor Thomas Stockmann
Enemy of the People

- 1 -

"Wonder where the hell he went," asked Azriel.

The rain was pouring hard. The thunder and lightning occurred closer together.

"I don't know, idiot, I tried to tell you earlier. There's something about him that's not adding up. Call it a gut feeling. A *guess*."

"Is that the same gut feeling that told you to feed Pastor Shane to zombies? I'm not interested in your gut feeling. I trust the vampire a lot more than I trust you."

"I know better than to cross you, Azriel. I know what you're *capable* of. I am the one who rotted in a safe for a year with nothing but my thoughts. Whatever sins I committed I've paid for them. You're lucky I don't do the same to you. I could, you know. Even with your mind powers. I bested you before, I'll do it again," said Finius flashing Azriel an arrogant grin.

"We'll see when this is over," said Azriel.

"A temporary alliance, then?"

"Do I have a choice? But you even *look* like you're up to your usual bullshit, and I seize control of your brain. And this time, you'll *stay* buried."

"Agreed. What do your mind powers do to the vampires?"

"I tried. Back in Chicago. Nothing happened except one of them turned into a bat, then turned right back."

"Not good. The only reason I knew you could stop the zombies was because your ancestor did it, and I guessed it'd be the same for you."

"Good guess."

"My guesses are almost always spot on. Look boy, we have to stop Rood from resurrecting all those vampires. We both know that. Ideas?"

"Actually, yes. I do have an idea. Don't know if it'll *work*, though. Let's hope my guessing is as good as yours."

"Indeed."

To make Azriel's plan work, they had to go back to Pastor Shane's church and hope Rood wasn't there. On the way they stopped by a storefront not far from the town square called *Pete Vincent's Clothing & Apparel.* It was Belasco's only clothing store. If they were going to die, it would be fully clothed and not naked. After they grabbed the few clothing items still left after three years of looters having their way in the ghost town, they headed straight for Pastor Shane's church and hoped what Azriel needed for his plan was there.

Azriel thought about Granny.

Was Finius right and the rest of his family was like her? Willing to betray on a dime? And what of the Predator Rood killed who said he was there to kill Azriel? Was that another family member?

All Azriel knew was, if he survived this and somehow stopped the vampire apocalypse, he would have to be extra cautious. It's astonishing that he went so many months without being found as it was. If Granny knew where he was the whole time, maybe other Predators did, too. Not a pleasant thought.

As they approached the church Azriel stopped before walking in the doors.

"Listen, these vampires know about this place. I can *feel* them close by. I think they are inside waiting for us."

"Good," said Finius, showing his devilish grin and gently sliding his fingers over the edge of the machete he took back from Rood.

There was something different about Finius. When Azriel originally met Finius, he had a natural dislike for him. Maybe it was his shady smile, or his arrogance, or the fact he has some zombie in him – and it was a reaction his Predator instincts had to his presence. The natural dislike was still there. But this time, Finius seemed less obnoxious. More serious and agreeable. It could be fear of what Azriel was capable of doing to him. Perhaps a little ass kissing. But he seemed more likable now. Almost. He didn't seem to be afraid of Azriel's mind powers, though. Which seemed strange.

We'll see, thought Azriel. *We'll see.*

They walked through the church and to the stairs that led down to the basement where the secret door was. As they jumped down past the broken staircase, they heard hissing and laughing.

"Welcome back!" came a voice. It was packed with vampires – including the two they didn't kill when they attacked Rood. They were crammed like rats in the room. Azriel figured Rood posted vampires there just in case, guessing if the two did escape they'd head for there to look for ways to kill him.

He was right, of course. It looked like Finius wasn't the only one good at guessing, Azriel concluded.

- 3 -

The fight was over in less than a minute.

Azriel and Finius were prepared this time and there was no Rood there to help his children vampires – all of who were far less powerful, strong, or fast. And this time Azriel was pissed. He let the anger out – his own "monster," he was starting to think of it as – that natural, instinctive anger that put him in a virtual berserker rage.

It did little good against Rood. Rood was too fast and strong and skilled. With Rood, it was almost as if Azriel's rage was used *against* him as Finius had done when they fought three years earlier in that shack with the explosives in Belasco Woods.

But this time, Azriel and Finius were fighting together.

They tore through the vampires in Pastor Shane's panic room. Finius's machete moved so fast in his skilled hands it was just flickers in their eyes. Azriel punched holes through their chests and pulled out their beating hearts. He also ripped off heads... crushed throats, detached limbs, and broke necks. He was again that force of nature that took down the entire were-monster party. His beer belly from living a sedentary life was slightly shrunken – as if his body was incrementally getting itself back into combat shape with each new encounter.

And, as usual, the more he fought, the more he *liked* it. And the more he liked it, the more viciously he fought. He was *enjoying* himself. And when they were done with the low-level vampires... when they got what they needed from Pastor Shane's library... he would enjoy killing Rood as well. And then, if it made sense, he'd take care of Finius.

Betrayal is a bitch, he thought.

Before they finished, the two vampires who survived before turned to bats and got away again. Azriel figured they were the cowardly ones. Or the smart ones. Or both.

The thunder grew louder. Azriel thought about his plan. They would need to hurry to execute it.

His idea was merely a theory. He didn't know if it'd work, and it sounded almost silly. But theory – even silly theory – was better than nothing.

- 4 -

Azriel and Finius cut the vampires into as many pieces as they could. Since they had no matches, garlic, or stakes to permanently kill them – they took the vampires' body parts to the bathroom. One piece at a time, they flushed body parts – toes, fingers, hearts, organs, anything small enough to fit – down the toilet.

"Go find what you're looking for," said Finius as he dropped an eyeball in the toilet and flushed it down with another load of vampire parts. "I'll finish up here. This should slow down any regeneration – assuming these weaker ones *can* regenerate. I don't think they'll spontaneously become whole like Rood did. But you never know..."

Azriel went back into the panic room. The door was broken off from when Mara tossed him through it. Papers and books were everywhere. There was a book on the table, opened. Azriel glanced at it.

It was about hell.

Why would Rood's vampires care about hell? Read up, boys, I'm going to be sending you there...

Azriel read the page the book was opened to carefully. It had descriptions of the four different words translated as "hell" in the Bible – Sheol, Hades, Gehenna, and Tartarus. Azriel remembered Pastor Shane teaching this when he was a kid. Pastor Shane said Sheol, Hades, and Tartarus were connected, not the same as the lake of fire everyone is familiar with. Tartarus was a special holding place for the fallen angels that sired the ☐ ephilim. He remembered Pastor Shane saying they were stuck there "in gloomy chains of darkness." Azriel remembered these sermons since they were some of the only parts of the Bible that excited him. He found most of the Bible tedious and boring. But he loved all the violent parts, and the passages about angels coming down and fucking human women. A fascination that was tied directly to his destiny as a Predator, it turned out.

Azriel walked away from the book and started looking at the shelves. He didn't have a lot of time. Since Rood wasn't hunting them that means he was probably focusing on his plan to resurrect all the dead vampires in the pit. There was something Azriel needed. And while it had nothing to do with hell, it would hopefully help Azriel send these vampires there.

It didn't take long for Azriel to find the book he was looking for. It was written in Latin by William of Newburg – the first zombie hunter, and who was also Finius and Pastor Shane's ancestor. Was he the first *vampire* hunter, too?

Azriel couldn't read Latin but luckily Finius could.

"Think it will work?" asked Finius flipping through the book.

"Probably not," said Azriel.

For the first time since the night he grabbed hold of Finius's brain and made the original zombie's head consume him body part by body part... Azriel saw genuine fear in Finius's face. That used car salesman smile was gone, as was that air of arrogance – like he knew something Azriel didn't.

They were partners whether they liked it or not.

The next stop was the quicksand pit.

They wasted more time than they planned getting the book Azriel needed and figured Rood was already there, hard at work resurrecting vampires. There were hundreds of them according to Fezziwig. Hundreds of powerful vampires were about to be resurrected with Rood's blood – which was now infused with Azriel's blood, making them presumably even more powerful than before – and giving them more Predator attributes.

They wasted more time than they planned getting the book Azriel needed and figured Rood was already there, hard at work resurrecting vampires. There were hundreds of them according to Fezziwig. Hundreds of powerful vampires were about to be resurrected with Rood's blood – which was now infused with Azriel's blood, making them presumably even more powerful than before – and giving them more Predator attributes.

It was a scary thought to Finius. He knew what *Azriel* – Azrael, the angel of the death, as some of his former colleagues in The Order called the boy – was capable of.

Just as Granny did.

Just as Pastor Shane did.

Just as the last few remaining members of The Order did – that secret society he once belonged to before he was excommunicated – did.

The boy had powers and abilities far in excess of what anyone thought he'd be capable of controlling. That was the theory, at least.

Maybe it was good his brother Shane neutered Azriel with those blue pills. After an entire year sitting in a safe with nothing but his thoughts... as he was painfully conscious the whole time... Finius finally understood why his brother did what he did. Why he was wrong about wanting to unleash Azriel's (*Azrael's*) full might on the evil in the world. If the boy turned astray... if he got drunk on his own power... he would be unstoppable. He would make an especially dangerous tool if the enemy used him. The rulers of the darkness of this world would use the boy if they could. Finius and Pastor Shane and their entire Order knew full well who ruled the world at this time. And Pastor Shane was the first to suggest the boy – who they realized was especially powerful and capable of great evil even as a newborn – could be used *against* them.

It was a blessing of sorts that Azriel's grasp of his own mental abilities and power were still so *feeble*. Finius knew Azriel should have been able to tear through Rood. Tear through the entire vampire horde about to be resurrected. Tear through anything that got in his way. But he was fat, out of practice, and out of shape. Even his ability to control Finius's hybrid-zombie mind was probably weaker than it was before.

I'm sure we'll be testing that little theory out soon...

But eventually that would change.

And maybe, just maybe, Pastor Shane's theory on Azriel possibly being the anti-christ would be proven correct?

Finius thought that notion was silly for many years.

He figured it foolish to not let the boy know who he was, and encourage him to go forth and complete his destiny killing monsters and helping mankind. But now, he had to wonder. The boy had humanity, unlike most of his Predator kind. But he was also capable of great *coldness and violence*...

"Finius, are you listening," said Azriel. Azriel had been talking to Finius while he was lost in his thoughts.

The quicksand pit was already infested with vampires in the process of being resurrected when they arrived. Some were in the middle of the pit regenerating and resurrecting... and some were fully *whole* – naked and cheering in the rain, free at last. The pit was completely barren now of the holy water infused quicksand, which had mysteriously drained. The only water in that pit was the rain pounding down and slowly trying to fill the pit up, even as the mysterious suction power in the middle where Rood was standing was sucking the water down. Every drop of the holy water residue must have been gone now, judging by the fact Rood and hundreds of vampires were not burning. There was just mud and Rood standing by a giant pile of skulls and vampire remains. The pile was several feet high and wide. Azriel and Finius both wondered if that could be where the mysterious drain was, under the bones? Like a whirlpool drags everything towards its opening, all the bones are gathered there, too big to go down the hole?

It must be, they thought.

It had to be.

It was the only thing that made sense.

Whatever was under that pile of skulls and vampire remains must be sucking all the water into it. Rood stood there, corncob pipe in his mouth, a slit in both his wrists, dropping his Predator-infused blood – now mingled with Azriel's – onto the bones. Each time a drop landed on one of the skulls or bones, he kicked it to the side and it started spontaneously resurrecting the vampire it belonged to.

Rood looked up at them and smiled.

He shouted over the sound of the rain, "Oh joy! You're back! Finius I don't know what *you're* made of, my friend. But you're a sneaky little devil, aren't you? Yes... and something tells me your blood will be just as special to me. Azriel what's that in your hand? A book? I certainly hope for your sakes you have more than *that* to fight with."

The rain beat off Rood's face and shoulders and head.

"Boys, *get* 'em !"

There were hundreds of vampires in the pit. They were as strong as

Rood was – and there was no way Azriel – still weakened from so much blood loss – and Finius could fight the entire horde.

All they had was a crazy plan.

A plan Azriel and Finius realized probably wouldn't work.

"Alrighty then, let's see what happens," said Finius, holding his machete with two hands as the hoard of vampires rushed towards them.

- 6 -

Dozens of vampires rushed up the side of the pit.

Most were still groggy from their resurrection, slipping on the mud, not quite able to scale the side. Many of them fell back down, tumbling to the bottom. A few were clawing their way up, getting stronger with each passing moment. Azriel's Predator instincts kicked in. He could barely concentrate through the rage and hate to use the book. His hands were shaking and his fingers slippery from the water.

More thunder. Another flash of lightning. The rain was pouring so hard it looked like a wall.

"Hurry Azzy-boy, do your thing!" said Finius.

Azriel opened the book to the page he had marked. Water beat down on it, obscuring his vision of the words on the page – *this shit better not smear!* – as thunder rolled ahead and lightning flashed in perfect unison. It felt to Azriel as if the weather was being affected by the action he was about to take. As he fumbled with the pages, his blood loss-weakened and clumsy fingers dropped the book into the mud and lost his place.

Balls!

Azriel picked it up and flipped through the pages.

He quickly found the dog-eared page.

The first of the vampires were now just twenty yards away – scaling the side of the pit so fast they'd be upon him and Finius in seconds. Finius ran towards them, hacking and slashing with his machete. The high ground gave him the advantage, making it easy to decapitate the closest one.

Another of the vampires grabbed Finius and pulled him down next to three others. They sank their long fangs into his neck. Finius screamed, but the thunder drowned out the sound.

Azriel readied himself to implement his plan.

He had to wait.

He had to be *patient*.

Timing was crucial. Finius was begging him to hurry.

Rood still had more vampires to resurrect. Azriel didn't think this would work unless they were *all* resurrected. He ran around the rim of the pit, dodging the attacking vampires like an unholy game of tag. Azriel was fast, but the vampires were as fast or even faster – as they regained their full composure and the grogginess from being resurrected disappeared.

Azriel knew he needed patience. It's the only way this would work. If Azriel had had the time to count, he would have counted over 700 vampires now in the pit that was at least 100 feet deep. It took the vampires a lot of effort to climb around the slippery banks.

Finally, Rood dropped blood on what looked to be the last skull and bone pile. Azriel watched it start regenerating into a whole vampire. He saw a big triangle shape of metal at Rood's feet. Rain was pounding off of it.

That must be the drain.

Just another few seconds...

He looked over at Finius who was back on his feet, holding his bleeding neck with one hand, and slashing at the vampires with his other. Two decapitated vampires lay at his feet.

"Azriel what are you waiting for, do it! DO IT NOW!"

More thunder rolled.

More lightning flashed.

Azriel hopped into the pit, sliding down the side to the bottom, jumping over several vampires who were trying to climb up to get him as he slid down the slopes. Rood was laughing. The sound from the rain was louder than ever as it picked up power. The lightning flashes made Rood's body look like a silhouette of a tall hulking figure with a captain's hat that was way too small for his head. All the vampires, as far as he could tell, were together inside the pit.

This was his only chance.

Azriel started reading from the book. He didn't understand a word of it. He didn't know what he was *saying*, but he knew what was being *said*.

As he read the passage the approaching vampires stopped, and started crying out in pain. Rood was hunched over, the pipe fell out of his fanged mouth, the smile on his face twisted into pure horror. Even though their bodies were drenched in rain, wisps of smoke rose off them. As Azriel finished the passage, with the rain pouring down, he and Finius watched the vampires writhing in pain, screaming in agony, their naked vampire bodies literally melting – including their *bones* – right before their eyes.

The vampire screams were terrible, awful, screeching sounds. They were so high pitched it sounded like they could shatter glass.

Rood's body – all their bodies – was reduced to nothing.

Azriel read the passages again. As he read, the thunder subsided, as if the sky itself *wanted* to hear the words, and was cheering Azriel on. When the smoke and vapors and mist cleared, there was nothing left of the vampires – not even bone.

They had done it. They had destroyed the vampires. They had stopped the vampire apocalypse.

All that was left of Rood was his clothing, the captain's hat, and that damn pipe. And, *thank God*, thought Azriel, there was no more tooting. Azriel's plan worked.

"I have to hand it to you Azzy-boy," said Finius rubbing the bite marks on his neck. "Your idea to turn the rain into *holy water* with that blessing passage worked like a charm. These bastards are all finally and truly dead."

- 7 -

"You think they're 'dead' dead?" said Azriel.

"I'd say so, yes, they're dead. There's nothing left. And even if there was, without Rood's blood to resurrect them they couldn't come back anyway." Finius kicked Rood's clothing around. There were no visible signs of Rood or his vampires anywhere. "I say we find Fezziwig and kill him now. While it's still raining. The rain is slowing down. Having holy water douse them was brilliant, boy. Let's strike at him, too, the same way, while we *can*. It's barely stronger than drizzling now."

"No."

"What do you mean no?"

"I told you. Fezziwig is off limits. He is on our side. He helped us. He saved my life. Unlike you, asshole, I don't do *betrayal*."

Finius laughed.

"An ally? A friend? A Predator befriending a vampire – the *head* vampire? You have to be joking. Suit yourself then, then I will do it myself."

"You'll do as I say Finius."

"Oh Azzy, do you really think you can stop me?"

Azriel pushed the mental switch in his head. He'd spent months practicing it and honing his ability before. It's how he caught Finius last time. But this time, it had no effect.

"Boy, what did you think I did all those months with nothing to do but think inside that safe?" said Finius. He wasn't using his mouth to talk, he was communicating with Azriel mind-to-mind.

"How the hell did you learn that *trick?"* said Azriel, trying to reply back via his mind.

Finius continued telepathically, *"It's simple, dummy. If there's one thing I'm good at it's sharpening my will. My mind. You got me that one time. I dreamed of escaping Azriel. You have no idea. I didn't know how, but I just knew I would. God was with me – I knew that much was true. I'm one of the people He uses to do His dirty work, see? So I practiced strengthening my thoughts and my mind. I'm now immune to your mind powers, idiot, and have since I realized I could speak to you like this, but didn't want to unless I had to. I hate revealing all my cards, as you know. Guess I was right again, eh? I'm off to find Fezziwig. I am betting he returned to his secret chamber from wherever he went off to earlier. You can come with and help, or stay the fuck out of my way. Understand?"*

Azriel rushed at Finius. Finius turned, pivoted, and dodged, leaving Azriel face first in the mud. He then kicked Azriel in the face and flung mud into his eyes, and kicked him down into the pit. Azriel tumbled to the bottom landing on a hard rock. His energy was up from his blood coming back, but he was still too weak and slow to take on Finius.

"You're lucky I don't have time to kill you now, or I would," shouted Finius from the top of the pit before running off.

Finius was fast. Even faster than Azriel when at his best.

How did Finius – a mortal man – gain these powers? It was a question Azriel had been asking since the day he met him, and saw Finius doing weird things like spin a knife on his finger like a top and fight and run faster than even he could.

It went beyond just the zombie in Finius. There was *more* to him. There had to be. The zombies never even had those kinds of abilities. What other gifts did Finius have?

Azriel got up. The rain started to taper off. He wasn't about to let Finius kill his friend and ran after him. Azriel made it to the town square fountain's secret door, ripped the trap door off, and hopped down into the room.

When he landed he saw Finius and Fezziwig fighting. Fezziwig no longer looked like the weak, old vampire he did before. He was taller, more muscular, and was fighting with one hand. His other hand held a half full blood bag. Azriel recognized it was the second blood bag Rood filled with his blood that he had put on the ground.

Fezziwig wasn't just taller and more powerful. He looked *younger*, too. He wasn't hunched over anymore. His chalk white skin was tight instead of wrinkled and sagging. His man boobs were gone, a strong, broad chest taking its place. Even his balding head looked full.

Fezziwig moved so fast, even Finius couldn't dodge any of his blows or punches. Within seconds Finius was on the ground, out cold. Fezziwig quickly, like a spider wrapping up a fly, bound Finius with some metal cables, then looked up at Azriel.

"The LORD said you'd be here to help. And for that I thank you, you little faggot," said Fezziwig. "Don't expect him to reward you, though. More likely he'll make you... *suffer*."

Before Azriel could say anything else, the vampire was upon him, beating him without mercy or pity, until he couldn't move.

Fezziwig then bound Azriel with the same metal cables he bound Finius with.

Azriel determined through the fog and pain from the beating Fezziwig gave him that, yes, Fezziwig *was* younger looking.

He also moved so fast it was like he *teleported.*

"The LORD has plans for you, Azriel," said Fezziwig. Blood drooled off his bottom lip. "Nasty, unpleasant... *painful...* plans. I just have to set him free first."

12
KING OF EGYPT

"I made the nations to shake at the sound of his fall, when I cast him down to hell with them that descend into the pit."

- Ezekiel 31:16

- 1 -

"Five thousand years on this planet… and I *finally* get what it means to 'have faith in the LORD'," said Fezziwig squeezing his fists and admiring his newly enlarged arms and body.

Fezziwig wiped the blood off his chin. "Azriel your blood tastes like *ass*. I can't believe it… all these years on the earth… all the knowledge I gained… all the monsters, vampires, and Predators I killed… and it never dawned on me to drink *Predator* blood. To think I would gain some of the power of those whose blood I drank! Why didn't the LORD tell me this? No matter. I'm setting him *free*. And you two faggots get a front row seat to it."

"Set God free… what are you talking about," said Azriel wriggling his body, flexing, and struggling to break out of the metal cables he was tied in. He was exhausted from the days' events. He was also still weak from having so much blood drained out of his body. He was easy pickings for Fezziwig to take down – especially in his souped-up new state.

Fezziwig laughed. His laugh was deeper than before. It was also less gravely and more youthful.

"Who said anything about *God*, faggot. I said the LORD. *My* LORD. The one who created me. It amuses me how stupid you are."

Azriel had no idea what Fezziwig was talking about.

"And what about you, zombie man?" said Fezziwig looking at Finius. "I know you suspected something. I could *see* it in your eyes. You are a lot smarter than the little faggot here. He was almost *too* easy to control. Getting him to trust me was child's play. I've been around so long that I can tell what pains a person just by looking in their eyes. Someone has daddy issues? They have a certain look. Someone full of regret? Their eyes betray them. Some little faggot bitch boy like Azriel hurt on by women? It was written all over his face.

"All I had to do was press on his pathetic insecurity. Give him some advice, let him think I sincerely want to help him, and presto – I'm a *friend*." He turned back towards Azriel. "I thought for sure I'd have to touch on your daddy issues. If we had time I could introduce you to him... it's the kind of family reunion he... craves. Look at you... so much anger, Azriel. Look at you. Even now I can see it running in your veins – like acid. Nobody is that angry without being damaged. And the more damaged you are, the *easier* you are to control."

Fezziwig laughed as Finius shot an "I told you so, moron" glance at Azriel.

Azriel said nothing. What could he say? Fezziwig was right. He was easily manipulated. He was still a naive kid, despite his growing power and rage and what he thought he knew about the world. It was an important lesson to learn. A lesson, it seemed, that would cost him his life.

Fezziwig turned back towards Finius and kicked his face. Orange-colored blood shot out of Finius's nose. "What's wrong zombie? Nothing *witty* to say? No insults? You Newburgh descendants are supposed to be *smarter* than this."

Finius cocked an eye up at Fezziwig.

"Oh, yes, I know all about who you are," said Fezziwig. "Your ancestor William of Newburg saddled me with quite the *problem*. I hate to admit it but he old faggot had persuasion skills. But you two? You're out of your league, boys. You two faggots probably knew something was off about my town before. Surely all the death and chaos and evil it attracts were in your faces. But you don't know what's here... what's *really* here, do you? You will, though. I'm going to introduce you two fudge packers to my father... the one who *created* me. The true LORD."

"Aw shit I can't believe I never figured this out before," said Finius.

"What?" said Azriel.

Fezziwig smiled: "You do know finally, don't you Zombie boy? All those hours your pitiful little fraternity spend reading your Bibles – how could you not know about my father... Abaddon."

- 2 -

Fezziwig continued drinking from the blood bag, grimacing as he forced down each swallow. He could only get a sip down at a time. Every time he swallowed the blood his stomach made a loud growling noise, as if it was fighting to *not* let the blood in. Rood left an entire pint of Azriel's blood in his torture room. It never occurred to Azriel to try to destroy it – even if he'd had the chance.

Abaddon.

Azriel recognized the name but had no context for it.

His mind rushed back to all the sermons Pastor Shane gave on the book of Revelation. Azriel enjoyed that book. All the talk about blood rising to the horse's bridle. All the talk about the decapitated saints getting their revenge. All the talk about violence, and death, and suffering. How could he not specifically remember the part about Abaddon? Then he realized why: Abaddon is talked about during the trumpets. No wonder. Azriel used to find it amusing to fart whenever Pastor Shane quoted the trumpets. He thought it hilarious at the time. He imagined Pastor Shane saying, *"Not so funny now, is it, dumb ass?"*

"My LORD has had a long time to think up ways to punish you. He is pissed. He wants his revenge. He wants back what's *his*.

"He had an entire kingdom when he walked the earth when he and his kin came down from the heavens. You faggots had no idea my father was here, underneath this very town, the whole time, rotting away in a dark pit, but still able to *influence* people to do his bidding. Talking to them. *Whispering* ideas to them, just like he does to me now. You all had your very own fallen angel perched on your shoulders. You think you two are here by accident? You think that zombie infestation was your idea, Finius? You're fools if you believe that. Nothing happens on accident in Belasco."

Fezziwig laughed.

He flexed his arms and felt his own biceps. He was obviously pleased with himself. And like Rood, he relished bragging to his captors. Loved talking. Loved hearing the sound of his own voice. Azriel thought these vampires were like villains right out of a comic book. They never shut up and loved to lecture. A weakness he hoped to exploit somehow.

"The LORD told me you'd be here Azriel. When I first founded this town, the door to the pit was sealed under the quicksand. He wasn't able to easily contact other people except by emotion and suggestion. Only I could hear him – because he is my creator, the one who *fathered* me. I was the first of all the fallen ones. But after you blew the woods up, the door was cracked just a bit. That crack allowed him to sometimes contact me across vast distances. And the more the holy water quicksand dissipated, the more clearly I could hear his voice. At first, I couldn't always make out what he wanted me to do. But he told me I'd need your help. I couldn't figure out what that meant. How would you help me and *why* would you?

"But now I get it. Rood was on to something that in almost 6,000 years I never figured out: Your blood gives my kind power. Raw power. My body... my energy levels... all my ailments... changed with just a few *drops* from your blood when I found this blood bag after you escaped Rood.

"Even though I despise you Azriel... I really must *thank* you. I can take a piss again without it hurting! Do you know how *long* it's been since I could do that? My hypertension – gone! My diabetes, I don't feel the numbness in my arms and legs anymore. My ass crack doesn't itch from that goddamn dermatitis. My *hemorrhoids* have disappeared. I had an *erection* earlier. An erection! I haven't been able to do that in years without drugs. And it's all because I was *patient* and obedient to my LORD. And now I'm going to release him from his prison.

"I can do this! I can open the doorway. There is no holy water blocking me now. And no Rood. Thank you for that, by the way, I appreciate you doing my *dirty* work. I don't think I could have beaten Rood on my own. Not before drinking your nasty, *disgusting* blood."

"You and Rood love to yap too much. It's worse than fighting you two."

"Amusing, Azriel. Amusing. Even now you try to talk tough. But kill you? Not a chance, faggot. I'm not allowed to yet. He says you're far more valuable alive. I can keep you alive for years... decades... tapping your blood... getting stronger, more powerful, a better servant to the LORD after I set him free," said Fezziwig.

He turned to Finius who was secretly working on getting free from his metal cables. The locks were like child's play for him – especially compared to the way Rood had him trussed up earlier. But he still needed some time.

"Did you know, the LORD – MY LORD – created the zombie, too?" said Fezziwig. "He created him to *mock* your Jesus who he knew would come. He'd heard *Enoch's* prophecy. My LORD's idea was to create something that couldn't die, even if your god killed everyone with the flood. As a zombie he was *already* dead. When I set the LORD loose his first act will be to free the zombies you buried in the pit. Both of them. Together we can turn half this world into undead – vampires and zombies working together like in the ancient times – in a matter of *days*. The world will be ours in just a few weeks. Think about this... one of the most powerful angelic beings leading an army of vampires and zombies... undead... feasting on and turning humans... other than a few we let live to feed on, there will be no live humans left! No *salvation* for anyone! There will be no planet left for your Jesus to save! Oh the plans my LORD has for this world... you can't imagine it. Just like it was last time... but *better*. And no flood will stop him."

"Tell me you have a better plan than *that*."

"Your arrogance amuses me, little Princess. Do you know what Abaddon did before your god *cheated* and sent the flood? Your god was betting on you humans doing the right thing. But that Adam... well, he was a *pussy* just like you. It's funny to think about that. You and him both listened to your women and devils instead of common sense. Look where it's gotten you? Your entire race was almost entirely polluted by the LORD and his brothers. I watched it. People practically *begged* me to turn them into vampires. They were willing to trade their *souls* for immortality. They eagerly asked to do my bidding and feed the other fallen ones like me roaming the lands. To learn our dark secrets. To have the forbidden information not meant for mankind. We corrupted literally *everyone* on the planet! Every man, woman, and child had our blood in them, our *genes*. Everyone was evil and violent. Only old-man Noah with his family were the exceptions.

"Did you know it took that old bastard Noah 500 years to find a wife we hadn't corrupted? One who was still 100% human? Can you believe that? There weren't any women left who hadn't been born with our *blood* or had given themselves over to the LORD and his brothers in marriage. None of us were allowed to kill Noah, though. He was protected. *Sealed.*

"There are some rules – red tape – we couldn't get around. But every time Noah wanted to take a wife, one of us or our fathers *took* her first. My LORD Abaddon and his brothers were so good at what they did… that it took God *cheating* to stop it. Cheating! And he said he would never do that again. So who outsmarted who? Abaddon did what even Lucifer never could do. He *outsmarted* God."

- 3 -

"What happens next then," asked Azriel.

This vampire loved talking even more than Rood did. Maybe it was in their blood as vampires to squawk on and on and on. Azriel did not know. But slippery old Finius was readying his own plan and needed time.

Azriel didn't know what made him angrier: That the vampire so easily manipulated him, or the fact Finius was right and he didn't listen to him – thinking Fezziwig was his friend. It was humiliating and frustrating. Azriel had not only let women bitch him up, but he was made the vampire's bitch, too. Had he listened to Finius and dragged Fezziwig's sleeping body into the sunlight before going to Rood, this whole thing would be over.

Balls!

"I'm taking you to him Azriel. He's anxious to meet you. But before we leave I want you to know, really know, what you're about to meet. The suffering you will experience. Hell Azriel, I almost feel *sorry* for you."

Azriel glared at the vampire. The vampire gazed back, then looked away. There was something in the boy's eyes that made Fezziwig, even now, drunk on power, stronger than any other vampire who'd ever walked the earth… nervous.

Yes, there was something about this boy. He was scary. Fezziwig wanted to kill him. Now. Before Azriel killed him. But the LORD said to wait and bring the boy to him.

"Your Ezekiel talked about my LORD Abaddon," said Fezziwig. "He called him the King of Egypt. And it's all true, I witnessed it. I was *there*. I barely escaped the judgment. But once I free the LORD there is no scenario we don't win. Abaddon will lead an army of vampires and zombies. His other brothers still stuck down there in the prison will help by taking human women and making them concubines to bare more monster-kind. I'm not just setting the LORD free – I am setting them *all* free."

Fezziwig took another sip from the blood bag, made a face of disgust, stuck his tongue out as if the air would help cleanse it of the taste, then coughed.

"*Yecht!* Your blood tastes so bad it *hurts*," said Fezziwig. "As I was saying… it's not just Abaddon I'm setting free. I'm setting them *all* free. All my LORD's brothers imprisoned with him. And it's because drinking your blood… your precious *nasty* tasting blood… has given me the power to do it. The LORD said the gate is very heavy – locked tight. No human or demon or vampire or monster can open it. Only one of his brothers can do it, he said. But I can – with your blood. He said your blood is *especially* potent. That if I drank it I would be almost as powerful as one of his kind – one of the *angels*. My LORD wants his kingdom back.

"He had it *all* before your God brought the flood. The LORD made me read and memorize what it says about him. He had the most wives and the most children – like me, nephilims, monsters as you faggots call us – and his kingdom was right near Eden. Right by where it all started – a paradise on earth! The irony is amusing, isn't it? He had a powerful kingdom so rich even the other fallen angels were *jealous*. He was the tallest and most powerful of the angels that came down. He had the most wives and the most wealth and the most food and controlled the most land. He *seized* whatever he wanted from man and angel alike. His children… his creations… like me and the zombie… we were his proudest delight. He didn't want to just create life by impregnating women… he wanted to turn the dead *into* the living. The living dead – vampires and zombies. No other angel could do that. Only he could. He controlled everything. Nothing else compared to my LORD's greatness. My zombie brother and I ate like kings. We *were* kings! People worshipped us along with our LORD – even offered themselves up to us as *sacrifices*."

Fezziwig shook his fists at the sky in triumph. Both Azriel and Finius thought he sounded like he was going mad.

"Then the flood came. The good times ended. Me and my zombie brother are the only ones who escaped it. The zombie was never alive to begin with and so couldn't really be killed – he was lost for centuries. Some of my vampire spawns found his head hundreds of years ago. I was supposed to meet up with him, plan our assault on the human race… but he was killed by *your* son of a bitch forefather."

Fezziwig pointed to Finius when he said "your."

"And to think I helped that William faggot afterwards, instead of staking beheading and setting his dumb ass on fire."

"The LORD spoke to me before you found me tonight after killing Rood. His voice was clearer than ever since that the crack in the door cleared. He told me he has been quietly influencing this town for decades. He has been manipulating and pulling the strings of the people – making them do his bidding, having his *fun* with them. The LORD has been waiting for the right opportunity to escape his cage. He knew when Rood decided to look for Predators he'd have his day. He knew of you, Azriel. Knows what you are capable of. He is wise and a genius and powerful. You are no match for his intellect."

"He must have been the one who resurrected Rood," said Finius to Azriel.

"Maybe you're not as stupid as I thought," said Fezziwig. "The LORD thought Rood would be more obedient. He tried speaking to Rood but Rood ignored him or simply didn't hear him, too caught up in his own lust for power. I was the good child! I was the one The LORD should have trusted. But kings always have their *prodigals*, don't they?

"The LORD even showed me how to *cheat* your God the same way your God was about to cheat him. He told me to go to the ark Noah was building when the animals were going in. Told me to become a bat. An unclean animal – and go in. I easily picked off the bat that was supposed to go and took its place. Your God allowed it. I have no idea why. But here I am, about to help rewrite his prophecy when I release Abaddon from the *Abyss*. You see, while all the flesh men-hybrids and animals died... God sent my LORD and his brothers into the pit. I did not fully understand it until reading the book in your Pastor Shane's church last night while you were fighting Rood. But now I get it. I know *where* the LORD is imprisoned now. And you're going to help me free him."

- 4 -

"Want to know how it all went down?" asked Fezziwig. He was quite enjoying lecturing the two. He'd missed being able to lecture someone since he killed Starr.

"I saw it happen," said Fezziwig. "I saw all of it... and what I didn't see, the LORD told me about. The flood changed the entire landscape. Valleys sank down and mountains rose up. There was a giant *whirlpool* that sucked everything – living and dead, angel and animal, Nephilim and monster, into a subterranean chamber. The ancients called it *Sheol*, the apostles and Greeks called the part of it where my LORD and his brothers are imprisoned *Tartarus*. The LORD told me all the other angels *fainted* when God imprisoned him and his brothers in there – the part reserved *just* for them.

- 5 –

"It's so funny to hear that word 'hell'," said Fezziwig. He picked Azriel and Fezziwig up by their metal cables and, with one effortless leap, jumped up and out of the room under the town square fountain.

Fezziwig was close to 10-feet tall now.

He carried Finius and Azriel like they were dolls.

"The LORD wants to *thank* you Azriel, for cracking the door. None of this would be possible without you. He hates you. Says your power is a threat to him. He says you're Lucifer's *favorite* – he's not supposed to touch you. But he appreciates your efforts that allowed this all to happen with that explosion you set off in the woods."

- 6 -

"It's true, you know," said Fezziwig, practically skipping along like a child. They were almost to the pit and he acted like a boy about to meet with his favorite sports celebrity.

"The LORD said the explosion you set off *cracked* the prison door just a little. Enough that it created a small pocket of air that for the last few years has been sucking in the quicksand and all the holy water. Whatever power your God set up to keep the hatch door from being opened, was sucking in all that sand.

"The LORD waited patiently until it was time for me to come down. He said Rood had to be destroyed. Rood's plans would *interfere* with his."

- 7 -

Azriel pressed on that mental switch in his head hoping it would do something to Fezziwig. But nothing was happening. Even if it just turned Fezziwig into a bat like one of the weak vampires in Chicago, that would be something, at least.

But he also knew they were in way over their head.

Monsters were one thing. But angelic beings? That was another.

And what was this about him being "Lucifer's favorite"? Azriel didn't like the sound of that at all.

He looked over at Finius. Usually you could not shut him up. But now he was silent.

"Hopefully you're ready to escape your binds," said Azriel, communicating with Finius in the same unexplainable manner they used when fighting in the pit.

"I need more time. You have a plan, I hope?"

"Yes..."

Azriel telepathically talked to Finius as they approached the pit. They formulated a plan. It was another long shot plan. It had even less a chance of working than the rain-into-holy-water plan.

And the odds were not in their favor.

But they had nothing to lose by trying.

"We're heeeeeeere," said Fezziwig.

13
DOWN THE HATCH

*" ...God did not spare angels when they sinned, but cast them
into hell and committed them to chains of gloomy darkness
to be kept until the judgment."*

- 2 Peter 2:4

- 1 -

"Dammit! I can't open it!" hollered Fezziwig.

His younger, louder, and ever deepening voice echoed off the pit's walls. They were in the center, at the large triangle hatch. Fezziwig was trying to pull up on it. But he had barely managed to get his fingers under the small crack from it being slightly moved off the hole it was covering.

"What's wrong, *Count Chokula*," mocked Azriel. He stopped trying to escape the metal cables Fezziwig tied him up in. Instead, he hoped to frustrate the vampire. Frustration could lead to mistakes, and mistakes could lead to Azriel's plan working.

The plan was all about timing.

If they didn't get the timing just right, the plan would fail.

What the hell are these made of, anyway, titanium? Azriel thought. They seemed stronger than the thick chains Rood tied him up in.

Azriel looked at Finius and they nodded at each other.

"Mock away you little faggot," said Fezziwig taking a break from trying to lift the hatch. He was out of breath and sweating. The effort – even in his powered-up form – was exhausting. "The LORD will *punish* you in ways that will make you wish your mother never squirted you out of her cunt."

"Not if you can't lift that hatch, Barnabas," said Azriel. Finius told him via their new telepathic link, that he still needed more time to escape his binds. Finius was a talented escape artist. But these bindings were much harder to get out of than he anticipated.

I still need more time, Azzy-boy, to escape these binds without him noticing. That way I can get into position at just the right moment you need me to. You just make sure you do your part.

All right. You will have you're time. Stand by.

"All this means is your blood I gagged down earlier isn't going to *cut* it. I'll need more juice to move this hatch. Fuck-a-duck I don't even know how that explosion moved it the *crack* it did. No matter. I'm just going to have to drain *all* your blood."

Fezziwig laughed and bared his teeth.

His fangs slowly grew down to his chin.

"Fezziwig… I swear to God, if you…"

"What are you going to do you little bastard," said Fezziwig, cutting Azriel off. "You can't even *touch* me much less fight me. You're so stupid. You have all this power locked inside you and don't even know how to use it. And the power you do have you wield like an *amateur*. The LORD says I should be cautious with you. Says you are capable of killing me. Even *now*. But he also said not to kill you. What choice do I have? I need *all* your blood to set him free."

Fezziwig clicked his teeth. The noise sounded metallic. Azriel was running out of ways to stall.

And what of his plan?

Azriel knew it probably wouldn't work. There were too many moving parts. Too many things had to happen at just the right time. It would require the vampire to lift the hatch up more than he had, but not enough where anything escaped the pit. It would also require some luck. But luck was a commodity Azriel figured he had already ran out of with his turn-rain-into-holy water trick.

Fezziwig looked at the mostly-drained blood bag and tossed it on the ground.

"Only a couple swallows left in there. I'm going to need a lot more," he said. "Your blood is going to taste like ass. And I don't know how much I can keep *down*. But I'm going to drain you. All the way. But first… *first*… I have to *piss*. Don't you two go anywhere. Stay right on that *spot*," Fezziwig laughed.

He started pissing right next to Azriel and Finius.

"Look! No more stage fright, either!"

Fezziwig's urine was pinkish and smelled like a dead animal. He didn't piss right onto them. But the stream landed closely enough where several drops ricocheted off the ground and landed on their shoulders and legs. In Azriel's case, one drop hit him in the cheek.

"Aaaaaahhhh," said Fezziwig holding his penis with one hand, the other on his thrust-out hip. "Do you know how long it's been since I could piss like this? Without waiting 15-minutes just to squeeze a few drops out? To not be piss-shy if people are around? To have a full stream and not just *dribbles*? Dear LORD, I love this!"

Fezziwig finished urinating and clicked his teeth again.

"Okay, faggot," he said looking at Azriel. "Time to do the *nasty*."

Fezziwig grimaced as he prepared for the sickening taste.

"Down the hatch!"

He opened his mouth wide, sunk his long fangs into Azriel's neck, and drank.

"I hope you *choke* on my blood you sick son of a bitch!" said Azriel, as blood ran down his neck in two lines. Fezziwig's drinking was sloppy and chaotic due to the taste. Some of it dribbled down his face and chin, but he was swallowing most of it.

The taste was even worse than before. Every few seconds he had to stop, lift his head up, and hold in his vomit. It was the worst taste he could ever imagine. But at the same time, with every drop he swallowed, he felt his body growing bigger, stronger, and more powerful, even as the blood incrementally tasted worse.

Dammit!

How could his blood taste even nastier than before?

Fezziwig's stomach wretched and heaved, as if it wanted to dispel the blood as soon as it drizzled down his throat. But he trudged on, keeping it down, repeating his cycle of stopping for a few seconds, holding vomit in, then sinking his teeth back into Azriel's jugular.

Fezziwig peeked over at Finius. He was still tied up.

Good. One less thing to think about.

As Fezziwig drank, the LORD told him what should be done to Finius. He said to keep him alive. He was not to be killed or violated. Fezziwig could do whatever else he wanted to Finius. But he was not permitted to kill him or turn him into a vampire – not that Fezziwig had any desire to do the latter. The LORD had special plans for the slick old man with the devilish grin. But what plans? And how would he fit into the vampire and zombie army the LORD wanted to build?

Only time would tell.

These thoughts helped keep Fezziwig's mind off the awful taste of Azriel's blood.

And what of the boy? He didn't scream. Didn't fidget. Didn't even make a sound after telling Fezziwig to choke. It's like he knew he was going to die and he was going to take it like a man – even if it was agonizing having all his blood sucked out one swallow at a time.

Maybe the little faggot is starting to sack up and quit being such a pussy after all, thought Fezziwig, still amused at how easily Azriel was manipulated.

Draining Azriel's blood took a lot longer than Fezziwig planned. But after several bouts of holding in vomit and gagging the blood down, the boy was tapped out. He lay completely motionless. His skin was whiter than before. His still-opened eyes had no light. His body was as stiff as any other corpse.

Fezziwig sat on the ground holding his stomach. He felt more raw power pulsating through his body than he ever could have imagined possible.

"Don't throw that blood up you old fucktard, don't you dare!," he told himself.

Fezziwig's stomach was so bloated it looked like he was pregnant with quadruplets. It wretched and heaved. The blood wanted out. Fezziwig could feel it. It did not want to be inside him. It was fighting him.

Fezziwig thought about how, wouldn't it be just like his bad luck to fuck up now, so close to achieving his mission? If he even so much as let himself *burp* he was afraid he'd toss up the precious blood digesting in his belly. It would be similar to the time he drank a hooker's blood (*the sex was incredible, but her blood tasted like it had* parasites *in it.*...) then got excruciating gas. He was sitting comfortably on his couch, feet up, ready to watch *Men At Work*, and decided to let a fart out. But instead of gas, he shit his pants. He then burped and threw up all over the shit stain he made on the couch cushion. The combo ruined the couch, stunk up the entire basement, and his concubine passed out from the nauseating stench. It was all he could do to finish the movie before doing something about the mess. He also had no clean underwear, and had to resort to turning the cushion over until they could find a new couch.

Thus, he refused to burp or even so much as move. He needed to give Azriel's blood – as it kicked and bucked to leave the vampire's body, like it knew it didn't *belong* there – time to be absorbed. He didn't think it would take long.

Whatever digestive juices were in a vampire's body helped him break down and digest blood fast. Until then, Fezziwig would will himself to keep the hostile blood down. The taste in his mouth was still repulsive. Maybe he could tap just a little of Finius's blood to cover the taste?

No, better not. Now was not the time to upset the LORD.

Minutes passed. Fezziwig felt the blood in his stomach being absorbed into his body. His belly was almost shrunk down to normal size. It was time. The power in his body was immense. He felt like he could punch a hole in a *mountain*.

Fezziwig stood up and realized he was higher off the ground.

He stood at least 15-feet tall.

His body was hard as a rock.

And he was so strong, every step caused a small *tremor* in the pit.

What the hell was *in* Azriel's blood? Whatever it was, was it enough to help him pry the mysterious metal triangle hatch all the way off the portal and let Abaddon – his LORD – free? He assumed it would. This will be first time the LORD will have walked the earth since before Noah's flood killed all the nephilims and sent him into the Abyss.

Fezziwig couldn't fail.

He wouldn't fail.

The LORD was counting on him.

And he knew the LORD didn't tolerate failure.

Fezziwig got on his knees again. He slipped his fingers (*even my fingers are stronger!*) under the open crack the slightly moved triangle-shaped metal hatch had created.

Time to give it another try.

On the count of three.

One… two…

His plan was to lift it up just enough to let the LORD out. Then the LORD could completely remove it. But could Fezziwig do it? It was damn heavy before. But now Fezziwig had all the blood of the supposedly most powerful Predator who had ever lived inside him.

Azriel's blood stopped kicking and screaming to leave Fezziwig's body. It was part of Fezziwig now. He could feel it racing through his veins.

Fezziwig tensed his entire body preparing to lift the hatch. He felt so strong he thought he'd crush the triangle hatch just touching it. His feet sunk into the dirt from the pressure his powerful steps made. Wisps of smoke rose from his footprints. The residual holy water that had seeped into the dirt was still affecting him. No matter, he thought. It was mostly harmless now. And the power that Azriel's blood gave him was unbelievable. He wished he could have kept the little faggot alive perpetually as the LORD intended, tapping Azriel's disgusting-tasting blood regularly, just enough volume to weaken him, but not kill him.

The boy healed fast, after all. Surely his body made blood faster than regular humans, too. It was an interesting fantasy. But, it wasn't going to happen.

The boy was dead.

The Predators were bred through the centuries since after the flood, when more fallen angels went to the earth's surface to impregnate human women, to be the perfect supernatural killing machines. It's probably why their blood tasted so horrible. It's why even though Azriel had his ass handed to him time and again that he was still able to keep going. It's why, now, Fezziwig was able to do one of the things Azriel's creators were trying to stop the whole time:

Release Fezziwig's LORD Abaddon.

"It is time, LORD. Time for you to walk the earth again!"

Fezziwig slowly lifted the metal triangle, which was less than a centimeter crooked off the hole it was covering. A sucking noise came from the crack that sounded like a vacuum. The suction was what was making it so hard to move. Despite Fezziwig's power, he still struggled to lift it. Whatever force sucked in all the quicksand, was working just as hard to keep the hatch shut.

Fezziwig lifted up again.

He lifted it just an inch, then dropped it back down, forcing him to relax and get his bearings. Then Fezziwig tried again and lifted it another centimeter than before, then dropped it again.

Fuck this!

It either lifts up or I die trying!

Fezziwig tensed his body to lift it again. This time he lifted it a bit higher than before. His hands shook, veins popped out of his arms and temples. He yelled as loud as he could. He sounded like a weight lifter maxing out on his bench press, trying to give himself every advantage.

"Arrrgghhh!" he yelled. He lifted it a full foot high. He thought he could even see movement inside the hole. He decided it was time to get under the hatch now, so he could push up, instead of straining his lower back trying to pull it up. As he dropped to his knees to get under the hatch and press it up, a large scorpion-looking tail poked out, like a periscope, whipping around.

Fezziwig smiled. Two more tails poked out. They slithered back and forth, like snakes. Fezziwig also heard other sounds – buzzing and what sounded like horse hoofs and lions growling – coming from inside the pit. What else was he hearing? Wings? Yes, buzzing wings, like locusts.

So it's true…

They are all down there…

And they want out…

Fezziwig felt his master's presence for the first time since before the great flood – when Abaddon was sucked down into the Abyss via another similar portal as the one he was standing over.

Or maybe this was where they were all sucked into… this spot, this town… maybe this was the only gate?

Or maybe not. Fezziwig heard there were seven such portals in the world.

But that was most likely pagan nonsense – with as much basis in reality as there being a hellmouth next to a high school in California. The pagans were always twisting the old truths. They were too stupid to create anything original – and simply told their own warped versions of the stories that really happened, complete with their own gods, heroes, and villains substituted in for the real ones.

Fezziwig pressed up hard. A streak of pain shot through his upper back. He ignored it. He was too close to let pain stop him. The hatch door was almost open now. Just a little further and he could heave it off. But he'd need to get his bearings first. He'd need to summon all the strength he could muster, while letting it rest on his shoulders. As he did this, he looked down at the hole.

The scorpion tails were gone.

He no longer heard horse hoofs and lion growls and flapping wings.

Instead, he only saw a pair of eyes and heard rustling chains.

He knew those eyes. They were his LORD's eyes. They were bright, and sinister, and full of triumph. There were also teeth... a smile. The teeth were perfectly white. The smile arrogant and regal. The mouth didn't move, but the LORD's voice was in Fezziwig's head.

It was the LORD!

Yes!

He was about to set his LORD free!

Just another few inches and the triangular hatch would be completely off. But the more Fezziwig moved it, the heavier it got. It made no sense. How does a hatch get heavier? Were other forces actively trying to stop him? According to prophecy the angel instructed to free Abaddon had a key to let him out. Maybe that angel was somehow making the hatch heavier...

Fezziwig was getting frustrated. Why wasn't this working faster?

"Best be careful," said a familiar voice from behind him.

Fezziwig turned his head.

His arms and body shook from holding the hatch up.

"You just got rid of those nasty hemorrhoids – be a pity if the strain flared them back up."

It was Finius.

- 4 -

Fezziwig tried holding the hatch door up with one hand and it dropped and rested on his shoulder. It was so heavy his arm felt like it was on fire. But he'd come so far. He couldn't let it close now and start over.

Finius jumped towards Fezziwig's head, and landed on his shoulders. Finius started trying to choke the old vampire out by wrapping his arms and legs around his neck. But Fezziwig's neck was packed with steel-like muscles after drinking Azriel's blood, and barely even felt Finius's grip. Fezziwig whipped his neck around left and right, up and down, trying to toss Finius off him.

No good.

Finius was too fast and had a vice-like grip of his own.

What is this guy made of?

Fezziwig decided to ignore Finius. He would swat this particular gnat later. For now, he would put all his strength into lifting the hatch door and letting Abaddon out.

As they struggled, both Fezziwig and Finius felt something invisible – like a frigid blast of air – come out of the pit. As it passed by them, an icy streak shot up their spines and a smell like brimstone filled their nostrils. The hairs on their arms, legs, and heads stood up. Something – two somethings, two *presences*, it felt like to Fezziwig – passed by them. Finius tried to ignore the sheer feeling of horror seizing his mind. Even Fezziwig look terrified. As the two presences passed, they both let out a sigh. Both were shaking uncontrollably from the fear. Fezziwig knew what they were – he'd had *dealings* with their kind before. They were invisible, non-corporeal, and evil. But they weren't trying to interfere and so he ignored them. He just wanted his LORD out. And once out, Abaddon would be able to open the door again and let his locust army and his fellow fallen angels in the pit free. Then they would resurrect all the vampires and the zombies, and recruit all the monsters of the world (*they dare not say no to my LORD*). Then the real war against God – the *real* Armageddon – would begin.

So go ahead Finius, you gnat, try to stop me.

What good will it do?

Fezziwig was so strong the hybrid man-zombie was having about as much effect on him as a fly would have on a human. Finius was annoying, but ultimately harmless. Fezziwig didn't even feel it when Finius hit and squeezed all the vulnerable areas that would normally knock a man out just by touching them.

But Fezziwig was no man.

Nor was he ordinary – not even for a vampire.

Not with Azriel's blood circulating in his veins giving him more power than had ever been possessed by a vampire. And since he was Abaddon's *first* child… the first ☐ ephilim… he would know.

"You're wasting your time, Finius. One more push and this door will be open enough to let the LORD out!"

Fezziwig braced his legs and back to press one more time. He looked down long enough where he could see black smoke – blacker than even the darkness inside – starting to gather in the hole. The smoke moved, but did not drift out. It was as if whatever strange force sucked in all the quicksand and was holding the portal hatch shut was keeping it in. His LORD's head poked through the smoke. His perfectly shaped angelic hands – shackled by chains made of a metal that looked both ancient and strong – reached up through the thick smoke and grabbed at the ground, digging his fingers in. Abaddon talked to Fezziwig not via telepathy anymore – but *audibly*.

"Hurry!"

The voice was chilling, and beautiful, and elegant, and evil at once.

Fezziwig would not fail his LORD.

He screamed into the clean night air.

He gave one last final push. Both his arms exerted every last ounce of strength he could muster.

In another few seconds the hatch would be off.

The LORD would be free.

Finius wasn't sure what else he could do.

He wrapped his arms and legs around the 15-foot tall vampire's neck and squeezed with all his might and barely indented Fezziwig's flesh.

He tried boxing Fezziwig's ears. He tried punching Fezziwig in special areas of the neck and face and temples – all those wonderfully painful pressure points – that would knock anyone else out cold instantly. He tried every trick he knew.

But nothing worked.

It was such an exercise in futility Fezziwig completely ignored him. He tried every way he knew to stop the vampire but had no effect. And Azriel was now dead.

Or was he?

Finius glanced at the ground and noticed Azriel's body was gone. Where did he go?

Finius looked around as Fezziwig was about to do his final press. He could feel all the muscles in Fezziwig's gigantic body tense. He saw Fezziwig's bare feet digging so hard into the ground they were nearly covered in dirt all the way to his ankles. Smoke appeared from where Fezziwig's feet were buried, touching that residual holy water still soaked into the ground. The old vampire ignored the pain.

Where was Azriel? Where did he go? The answer was, he was right below them – concentrating, his hands on his temples. The boy was chalk white and looked like he could barely stand.

Finius heard a voice inside his head. It was Azriel's.

"It's game time. Don't fuck this up."

"Understood!" replied Finius.

Finius released Fezziwig's neck just as his body started to press up on the hatch door, and dropped to the ground. At that moment, anyone looking in on the fight would have thought Fezziwig seemingly disappeared.

But he didn't.

Instead, he'd been turned into a bat.

In the split second the door started to slam shut, the angelic arm with the chains – Abaddon no doubt realizing what was about to happen – slid back in. And Finius, knowing the plan, kicked – with his precision-perfect way only he could do – the bat-mobile Fezziwig down into the portal. The hatch door slammed shut completely, and perfectly aligned itself completely covering the hole, as if the door had its own awareness.

Not even a crack was showing now.

Fezziwig was trapped inside with Abaddon and his minions.

Then there was silence.

Finius and Azriel suspected Fezziwig would not be greeted warmly for his failure. For a moment – and only a moment – Azriel almost felt *sorry* for the old vampire.

- 6 -

"Cutting it a little close, don't you think?" said Finius.

"Yeah well, when you have all the blood drained out of *your* body, see how well your mind functions," said Azriel. He collapsed to the ground exhausted. He was pale. His blood count was so low he shouldn't have been alive, but was.

"How did you do it?"

"I don't know. Something *changed* when I regained consciousness. Maybe it was my mind's way of protecting me. I have no idea. I've been rusty over the past couple years. Couldn't even control your mind earlier today, remember?"

"Yes," said Finius with a sly look on his face. Azriel didn't notice it because he was still too weak and exhausted from lack of blood. His body was generating new blood rapidly and he could feel it rushing back into his system, pumping through his heart and into his brain.

But he wasn't 100% yet.

He was still weak and on his knees, hands on his hips, exhausted.

"So now what," said Azriel.

"Now what, what?" replied Finius.

"This portal door. It's naked out here. There's no quicksand covering it. No holy water. What if someone… or *something*… else wants to try opening it?"

"I think, Azzy boy," said Finius, "It's time to bring this town back to life."

- 7 -

Finius's plan was simple:

One of them would stay and watch over the town. There was pure evil underneath the surface. Not just what might be left of any vampire remains, but also the Biblical Abyss itself.

It all made sense to them now.

It made sense why Belasco was such a magnet for evil and strife. Why even good people turned bad in such a small, unassuming town. Why bad and evil men were *attracted* to it like unholy moths to an unholy flame.

Azriel witnessed it most of his life.

When he was told what he was, he thought it was his fault. After all, Pastor Shane said as a Predator, monsters and evil would be drawn to him, just as he would be drawn to monsters – like cobras fighting mongooses.

But it was more than that.

Finius was right as far as Azriel was concerned. Someone needed to stay there and watch over it. Someone had to make sure nobody – or no *thing* – tried opening that portal again – assuming it was possible. Fezziwig had to drain all of Azriel's blood in order to move it the small amount he did.

But Finius knew better.

He explained to Azriel there were other evil, dark things out there.

Things possibly even stronger and more dangerous than what Fezziwig had become.

These monsters were everywhere – in big cities and small towns alike. Azriel saw it in Chicago, where an entire subculture of were-monsters existed. It was possible someone knew about this portal. Would have heard it's exposed. Would be coming *back*.

They decided it was best if Finius stayed.

Azriel attracted the wrong things to him.

They also agreed it best Azriel get as far away from Belasco as possible.

14
THE GAME BEGINS

"I may be bad, but I feel… good."

- Sheila
Army of Darkness

- 1 -

Azriel made his way to the intersection of Anders and Hove streets and took the side path to the main road towards Radu Falls – the next town over, 27 miles away. It had a bus that would take him to Chicago.

He felt exposed walking along the highway. Almost paranoid. He couldn't stop thinking about what Rood said, how a Predator came to kill him.

How many wanted him dead? And, even more importantly, which ones knew where he was? Granny obviously found him – and kept tabs on him, even followed him on his date with Mina.

Mina, he thought.

Another chick dies simply because she was with you, Stupid Azz.

He lifted his shirt, looked at his belly, and rubbed it. The skin Rood tore off to make that sailboat was healed – barely even a scar remained. His neck wound from Fezziwig biting him was mostly healed as well.

The police would no doubt want to question him. And he'd have to be careful when he got back home.

He'd also have to be on the move again. But there were some things he needed from his apartment first. Chances are the police hadn't barged in there yet. It hadn't even been enough time to file a missing person's report. But since his date was missing – *just ashes in a dumpster* – and the last person she was seen with – him – was missing, too, they'd no doubt consider him a prime suspect.

Just when he was getting everything in place: Working a good business. Dating hot girls. Making great money... and he had even picked up some advice about girls from Fezziwig, ironically enough, that he could use.

Balls.

What would he do for money now? He couldn't go back to his old clients or his old life. Even if he created a new pen name, there were ways to trace things back to his last identity. How far up in the chain did the Predators and monsters go?

Azriel's mind ran on and on about these questions. And the longer it ran, the more paranoid he got. But that was a good thing. Look what happened when he got complacent.

He was going to be on the run again and would have to trash his name. The name on his driver's license he had changed via back door channels – Simon Harrelson – had to go.

Sorry Simon, you gotta die, too.

He decided go back to his original name Azriel. He was surely considered missing, along with the rest of the citizens of Belasco three years ago when the entire town was blown up. He still had his identity and papers from when he used that name before, so why not? It'd be a hell of a lot cheaper than buying a new one again. It might also draw anyone tracking him who knew his name to him, instead of him having to figure out where to find them. At least that would keep him from getting complacent.

Another thought: Finius would have his hands full re-building Belasco. Who would want to buy property in such a town, much less stop by and visit it? What a shit hole town. And evil.

The only thing worse than a shit hole town, is an evil shit hole town, he decided. Everyone in it died in a mysterious fire. (*That Abaddon bastard no doubt smiling the whole time*, he thought.) The quicksand pit it was known for was gone. And people had been mysteriously missing when they visited over the last several months, thanks to Rood and his vampires.

What did Rood call them?

Third generation – tier 3 – vampires?

Azriel thought they had killed most of the remaining ones from Rood's band. But there were so many it'd be hard to tell. Just another reason to sleep with one eye open. Finius would hopefully find and kill any leftovers. He would *sniff them out*, were his exact words. Whatever that meant.

Finius was creepy like that.

Slippery.

Azriel agreed with Granny about that – the man was definitely slippery.

He decided he would keep an eye on Finius from a distance and check in when least expected. Because if there was one thing about Finius you could count on, it was you couldn't trust him.

- 2 -

"All right laddy-bucks, who's first?" said Finius, as he entered the Belasco Police Department jail.

He'd spent the day finding and capturing the rest of the tier 3 vampires. He and Azriel killed most of them before, and there were only two left. Finius tracked them down, cornered them in their resting place, and captured them, then put them in the jail. They tried escaping by turning into bats, but that didn't do them any good as far as leaving the room. When

Finius came back in to check on them and saw they were bats he was not pleased. With a speed that defied anything the two vampires had ever seen, Finius captured them both and snipped off their wings with a big pair of scissors. It had no visible effect on them when in their vampire forms. But their bat forms were now permanently crippled.

Finius hated vampires.

He especially hated the way they *smelled*.

Ever since he had caught a baby werewolf several years earlier, drank its blood… he had a bloodhound-like sense of smell. That was the only attribute he got from the werewolf. When he had earlier figured out how to cure himself of becoming a full zombie, he discovered he could get a monster's attributes, but not all of them. In this case, he'd have preferred having its ferocious strength. But the sense of smell was a good thing, as far as he was concerned. He didn't want to turn into an animal during full moons any more than he wanted to crave human flesh from his zombie make up.

His sense of smell was incredibly useful.

It let him find things and people.

It helped him track child Azriel from one town to the next from Oregon to Illinois. It helped him track down Dr. Romero who made the blue pills, so he could kill him. (A mistake, in hindsight, Finius realized, as he had no leverage over Azriel or the other Predators now that nobody knew how to make those blue pills anymore). It even helped him track Azriel and Fezziwig when they hid from Rood in the room under the town square.

And now he used it to track down the last two tier 3 vampires.

"You two lovelies are my next project. Here is what is going to happen. First, I'm going to drain the blood from your bodies. Then I'm going to let you die in this room. Can't have you getting away and coming after me again some day. Or, worse, telling anyone *else* about me. No, that wouldn't do at all, I'm afraid."

"But you said you'd *cure* us. Make us human again!" said one of the vampires.

That was true. Finius promised to make them human again so they would stop trying to escape. A tier 3 vampire's existence without a stronger vampire to guide him through the world, and deal with a vampire's vulnerabilities and weaknesses, was not a pleasant one.

"And I will. A promise is a promise," answered Finius. "By draining all your blood and letting you starve to death, you will be human again. Human *corpses*, at least. But human as human can be all the same."

Finius reached into the cell, grabbed the first vampire by his throat, pulled him close to the bars, drove a needle into its neck, and proceeded to bleed it via a catheter into a large plastic bag.

When he was done with that vampire he did the same to the second vampire. After he drained their blood and left their carcasses in the cells he smiled. He delighted at the thought of what *goodies* he'd get from them.

- 3 -

Azriel made it back to Chicago near midnight.

The streets were thinned out with just a few bums laying in corners fast asleep, hands still cupped and stretched out for money. He decided to enter his apartment building from the fire escape. He didn't think there would be cops there yet. But, you never knew.

He wasn't scared of going to jail or being captured. He could easily take down cops or outrun them or get away even if he was caught. What he was scared of was being *identified*. Of being seen.

He would rather the cops think he was killed and missing, too, along with Mina, whose body Granny insisted they destroy with the other vampires that attacked them in the alley. After all, she'd been killed by a vampire bite. She could have come back as a vampire – albeit a weak fourth-generation vampire. Probably barely even able to grow fangs. But still...

It wasn't a perfect plan. But, it was all he had. And before he left he would need traveling cash.

Azriel scaled the fire escape. His belly wasn't poking out as far as it had, but he was still easily winded. Just another reminder he needed to get in shape. He needed to put the candy and booze and beer away. He needed to get healthy. He needed to start learning how to use his abilities, not let them go dormant. His life depended on it. Besides the fact there were other Predators and monsters seeking him out – it was just flat out more *convenient* not having to hold his breath when tying his shoelaces, or not worrying about being winded when climbing stairs.

He reached his bedroom window. No lights were on. He could see past the bedroom door and caught a glimpse of his front door. It looked intact. A thought occurred to him someone – or some *thing* – could be in there waiting for him. Maybe a Predator wanting to kill him. Or, what about that werewolf that threatened him before running off?

Balls.

He had started to forget all about those were-monsters. He practically invited them to come find him. What was he thinking?

At the time he was in a blood lust rage. He couldn't even remember everything he said except that he'd be back to finish the rest of them off.

Azriel climbed into his window. His heart was beating so hard he could hear it. He didn't feel any evil presence. So that was good. But a Predator wouldn't have one, most likely, so he stayed alert.

He scanned for the large *kangaroo* figurine next to the couch. He hid over $15,000 dollars cash inside in various denominations. At least some small part of him was still on full alert the last few years. He was ready to have to bolt at a moment's notice. It was a byproduct of when he first left Belasco and was wisely paranoid.

But that was before life got so cushy. Before the *vampires* attacked. Never again would he let himself get out of shape like this or complacent.

His life depended on it.

And, what's that saying – *only the paranoid survive*? Azriel took the money out. It wasn't a fortune, but it'd get him where he wanted to go: Home.

But not to Belasco. No, he'd go to his first home – or, at least, near it.

- 4 -

When Finius finished drinking the vampire blood – he looked at the now-empty blood bag Fezziwig hadn't finished, when the vampire decided to toss it and drink directly from Azriel's neck. Finius grabbed it afterwards, when Azriel wasn't paying attention. He had been dreading drinking it and putting it off. It smelled nasty.

The boy was a fool.

Finius hoped he wouldn't gain *that* attribute from Azriel's blood. There wasn't much left in the bag. Maybe a couple mouthfuls.

He had to drink an entire *gallon* of werewolf blood to get his heightened sense of smell. He assumed he would need a lot more of Azriel's blood if he wanted any of his mojo. But he'd take what he could get.

The boy may still be naive, but he was becoming more powerful... stronger... faster... even being out of shape as he was. And more *cunning*. Even more cunning than before. It was part of his heritage and his birthright. His parents were special, too. Pastor Shane and Finius and all of the members of The Order knew it.

Some of them wanted to destroy the boy upon birth. But they decided they weren't executioners. They weren't Predators and weren't going to kill a defenseless baby – even if Lucifer had marked him as his. How would that make them any better than the very monsters that tormented the world?

Finius thought about The Order.

Finius couldn't help but smile when he thought of them. A bunch of old, self-righteous holy fools. Well, most of them were holy. That Gibson was a lot more fun than the rest despite his obnoxious personality.

Finius stared at the blood bag. He would have preferred more than a couple swallows. But this would do for now. He braced himself for what would surely be an awful taste. He opened his mouth and fangs now mysteriously protruded from his mouth. They were attributes he just took from the third-generation vampires (how he would have liked to drink

Fezziwig's or *Rood's* blood…)

Azriel's blood tasted even worse than Finius thought. No wonder Fezziwig took so much time to consume it all. Just the small amount Finius drank was enough to make a rodent *sick*. As soon as it hit Finius's stomach, his body wanted to reject it. It bubbled and swished in his stomach. It took all of Finius's will power to keep it down. He wanted so badly to throw it up. It physically hurt and was like drinking scalding hot liquid.

Oh, yeah, he thought, as his body absorbed the blood.

The power…

The pain and taste was worth it.

Yes, it was *worth* it!

- 5 -

Azriel decided to leave Chicago on foot and thumb a ride out of state. The fewer people who saw him, the better – including people riding public transportation. In addition, the city was crawling with monsters.

Granny said they were all over, and normally they would have made a move on Azriel but were *scared* of him.

All the monsters were.

His antics in Belasco with the zombies demonstrated his power. Showed the monster society what he was capable of. So they laid low – at least, the ones who were organized did. At the time, Azriel had wondered why they looked so scared and it made perfect sense: They feared him.

And he would use that fear against them when he decided to start taking them down one at a time. He could no longer avoid his heritage. It was time to embrace it. Time to begin the *game*.

He would do what he was born to do. Not because of some sense of duty, but because he really enjoyed killing monsters. He loved it. He looked forward to it. He would be doing it right now if he could.

But he needed to sneak away for a while.

He needed to make sure he wasn't on any radars.

He needed to get back in *shape*, and get his head on straight.

He also needed to disappear from the city. He met Mina online months earlier. Surely they would pull his profile up which had his picture. Just one picture, though. And it showed a face thick from partying and eating and drinking so much. Once he got back down to his regular size he would look different. Maybe he would let his hair grow out longer, too.

He'd probably fit in better where he was heading anyway.

And if the paranoia really got to him, he'd grow a neck beard too, like the locals. That was the style where he was going, after all, he thought, as the bus crossed from Idaho into Oregon. He thought of going to one of the early towns he lived in called Barbra. But that would be no good.

He was unwelcome in Barbra.

And if anyone recognized him he'd be right back on the radar. He doubted the citizens there forgot about the boy who terrorized the other kids in the sandbox. The kid who nearly killed those two boys after he accidentally pulled their cousin's pants down and they menaced him. The kid who held a sharp piece of glass up to the girl's mom's jugular, and threw the glass piece so hard, and with such perfect precision, it stuck into the tree.

It creeped out the entire town.

It creeped out Azriel's mom.

It even now, years later, kinda' creeped out Azriel.

No, he wouldn't go to Barbra.

He had another idea. Small towns were great for hiding. Lots of people moved to small towns for that reason. It was just how it was. But even better than a small town is a small *seaside* town.

Seaside port towns were full of drifters.

Full of people other people avoided.

Full of their own dark secrets.

Perfect for a guy like Azriel.

- 6 -

Jacked up on Azriel's blood, Finius felt an overwhelming surge of strength and power. His arms, his legs, his back – they all felt like *steel*. He also felt a new sense of violence. His temper flared at the slightest thought of anything that annoyed him. He would need to get that under check. It was the boy's undoing every time they had fought – allowing him to use Azriel's anger against him.

Is this how the boy feels all the time?

So... angry?

So violent?

So furious?

No wonder he's so dangerous. No wonder he's so… powerful.

When Finius shacked up with Granny years earlier, he went along with all the kinky things the old hag requested. She was strong, too. She liked it rough. She damn near broke Finius's back. Finius had to take a lot of Viagra to get an erection to fuck her. She looked hideous. Her tits were like deflated balloons. And her body looked like a cadaver. She was especially fond of using her *tongue*. It was disgusting. Finius couldn't figure out how it was even possible for her to have that kind of sex drive at that age.

But rough sex is what she wanted.

And, it just so happened Finius did, too. Although not for the same reasons she did. She wanted some fun. But he wanted some of her *blood*. He wanted to consume it. To gain her Predator attributes – or, at least, as many as he could. It worked. After drinking from her neck as they role-played vampires, his agility and speed and coordination doubled.

He was able to move faster than anything else he fought. He was able to do acrobatic type moves usually only possible in cartoons. He was able to do parlor tricks like spin knives on the tips of his fingers like a top. People always got a kick out of that.

But now that he had Azriel's blood he felt more powerful than ever. He also felt a new mental "switch" in his mind form. It had never been there before. But he knew enough about it from Azriel that it was what controlled his mind mojo. It's what allowed Azriel to control the zombies by mind, turn vampires into bats, and what else?

Finius would have fun finding out. Oh, yes, he would have *lots* of fun finding out.

But first, he had business to conduct. He was being called back to the pit. There was a voice inside his head that wouldn't shut up. He heard it briefly when trying to stop Fezziwig from opening the portal. He also caught a glimpse of Abaddon's face, his smile, his evil eyes. At first he thought that voice was a byproduct of the blood he'd drank. But it was more than that. It was in his head, but it sounded audible... like a whisper behind a crack in a door. The voice told him to go to the triangle hatch that led down to the Abyss.

Finius had to go.

He had so many questions. There were so many riddles needing to be solved.

Apparently Abaddon still had a little bit of influence on the outside world even without the door being cracked open. Not much influence. But he could communicate with his children. And Finius was Abaddon's child by *adoption* since he had both zombie and vampire blood in his veins.

The voice told him it had answers to his questions.

To come speak with him.

To have a... *friendly chat.*

Finius agreed.

The voice told Finius how it was Granny who freed him from his safe in the shallow quicksand – wanting his help to kill Rood. She had been watching Azriel, knew which safe Finius was imprisoned in, and where Azriel had tossed it. She had been there when he did it – quietly, unseen, keeping in the shadows, not wanting Azriel to know of her existence. But when she saw Finius was just a head and a body, and it didn't reattach itself right away, she figured it was a lost cause and left him there.

Abaddon then told Finius how he was the one that resurrected Rood when the family with the boat came to town, and found the sack with Rood's remains and removed it from the shallow quicksand. Abaddon's influence was weak, but with the holy water and quicksand draining, and a crack in the hatch, he was able to resurrect his evil, black sheep child. He wanted Rood to do the deed of freeing him, but realized he was too unruly and disobedient. Too unpredictable. And too stubborn to even listen. So he told his first born, Fezziwig, to come down to achieve his two missions: To kill Rood and open his portal, instead. It was harder to contact Fezziwig since he was so far away. But eventually he was able to do it.

And lastly, the voice told Finius his plans.

A war was coming.

Finius, if he chose, could be Abaddon's first in command.

Fezziwig was supposed to do that, but he failed. Fezziwig was now being punished and tormented for his failure. The angels in the Abyss are *fileting* him even now. The voice said it wanted the boy Azriel dead, although it was against his master's instructions. The Sons of God in the pit were on Finius's side – rooting for *him*, not Azriel, to win. The voice said Finius was to leave the boy alone for now. Finius was too valuable to be killed at this point. The boy is Lucifer's *favorite*, but Finius is Abaddon's favorite. Finius needed to be stronger before trying to defeat the boy. Instead, the voice said, it was sending "specialists" to deal with the Predator. They will kill him.

Finius asked the voice why he should help it.

What was in it for Finius?

Because, said the voice, Finius was beyond redemption. He had done too many wicked things. There wasn't enough forgiveness in the universe for someone like him.

He was a traitor, and a murderer dozens of times over.

He killed his own parents. He killed some of his fellow kin in The Order. He killed Pastor Shane – who was a true man of God. He even killed an entire town, by creating the events that led to Chief Rawger becoming a zombie and all its repercussions, including the rise of the vampires.

And since Finius had mingled himself with Nephilim blood – becoming a hybrid of multiple kinds of monsters – he wiped out any chance of an afterlife. There is no resurrection for Nephilim. At least helping Abaddon and his master – as even Abaddon has a master – he would have a *chance* at escaping the fires of hell they were all destined for if their plans against God worked.

Finius listened to the ancient and seductive voice.

And he understood it.

And he believed it.

And he agreed with it.

There was no redemption for Finius – the game for him had now begun, and he had no choice but to listen to his new god, his new master and LORD – Abaddon – and do as he said. Joining with this devil was, ironically, the only way he would avoid hell.

- 7 -

Six months later, Azriel ended up in in DaBeach, Oregon – a port town on the southern coast, not far from the California border.

He picked DaBeach because it was small – just 2,000 people – and was off the beaten path, even though Highway 101 ran through it. He liked the town instantly. It was completely isolated from the rest of the world, quiet, and sparsely populated. He heard a woman at the market tell a tourist how this town was the hardest part of the United States to get supplies to.

Best of all: nobody wanted to talk to him.

He minded his own business and the locals minded theirs.

Azriel found a job cleaning fish. He never did let his hair and beard grow, but he lost his excess weight, and didn't look anything like he had while living his plush existence in Chicago.

The town had two types of people: retirees (the joke he heard around town was *'people come here to die'*) and drifters like him – passing through on foot, or who moved there to get away from big crowds.

It was the most beautiful spot Azriel could imagine and the sun was out a lot more than other parts of the state and coast he'd seen. That was because, he was told, DaBeach was in a banana belt. It had the most sun of any coastal town in the Pacific Northwest. Surprisingly, most of the beach was not crowded. It was too cold to swim in and the waves weren't big enough for surfing. Azriel hardly ever saw more than a couple people at a time on the beach outside the little one bedroom cottage he rented.

He spent his days cleaning fish and his nights trying to keep busy. He dared not take on any more online advertising clients. That life was no longer an option – even with the anonymity of the Internet.

But Azriel still had his temper and anger to contend with. Sometimes he thought about Kerry Ditzler being raped or his mom being violated by Chief Rawger... or Mina having her throat ripped out... or any of the many atrocities he saw, and he'd break something.

It started off with him breaking an alarm clock or something small. Then it turned into punching holes in walls. Then, when it got really bad, he flipped the old rusty car he bought for just $500 over one night.

He needed an outlet for his angst and anger. He used to quell it with sugar and alcohol. He was a happy drunk, not a mean one, and in fact, never even wanted to fight when drunk.

But he didn't want to go back down that road.

He wanted to be healthy. He needed to be. He couldn't let his guard down even for a second. So he decided to do the next best thing: write stories.

He still loved writing and telling stories and his stories were always violent. They seemed to give him an outlet for his violent urges and thoughts.

He sensed no monsters around. That was good for now. But eventually he knew he'd be sucked back into the *game*. And he'd have to play his part.

As Granny told him: he was a player in a bigger game and he could no longer sit on the bench. How and when and why he would get back in the game he didn't know. He enjoyed his new existence. He no longer cared about going back to Chicago to wipe out the were-monsters. He didn't care anymore what Finius was up to – although he knew the old shyster was up to something. He didn't even care about fighting monsters.

But he knew, deep down in his gut, people like him were not meant to have peace. He was not meant to have a happy ending. He knew he would die a bloody, horrible, painful death. He could feel it. Sometimes he even drew detailed pictures of someone burning to death in a large furnace, screaming, writhing in agony as unseen entities laughed and cheered it on. It was almost like he could *see* it happening in his brain as he wrote. He would also dream about what he was drawing happening, at night but could never tell who it was burning. Was it him? Or someone else?

Some nights he'd get bored of writing. Get bored of watching TV. Get bored of sitting around or even walking the beach which he loved doing.

So he'd visit a local tavern down the street known by all the tourists as having the Northwest coast's best margaritas. But even with its popularity, it was usually mostly empty except during tourist season. Azriel wondered how it even stayed in business. The bartender/owner was named Jackson and was a decent fellow. Azriel tipped him well. On occasion, Jackson tried talking to Azriel. But Azriel was his usual standoffish self. He didn't want any more friends or attachments. Every time he had a friend or girl in his life, they either died or betrayed him.

Azriel became a regular as the weeks passed. He liked that it was quiet in there. He liked that nobody asked him questions anymore. He liked that he could go in with his laptop and write stories while having a cool beverage. He continued to write stories about monsters and evil beings. The first story he wrote was about a demon possessing and killing people. He found himself reading the Bible a lot – specifically about the nephilim tribes and how Jesus cast out demons.

Why was he always thinking about these specific things? Maybe there was a reason.... maybe there wasn't. Who knew?

He paid cash for his drinks (mostly lemonade or the occasional Pepsi). He no longer cared for booze, or candy, or beer.

His paranoia got worse. He knew by using his original name he was inviting people to find him. But that was good. He would rather his enemies come to him.

And while he never felt the internal radar that sounded when around monsters, he always felt like someone was *searching* for him. He sometimes woke up in the middle of the night and checked the doors and windows.

One evening, as he walked into the tavern after living relatively happily and comfortably in DaBeach for nine months, his peace streak abruptly ended.

He was sitting alone drafting a short story about an owl with insomnia when an unusually tall, manly-looking woman sat next to him. The woman was dressed in a tank top, shorts, and had a blond flattop haircut. She was abnormally muscular. Her legs looked like logs and her arms were like steel poles. Her face was devoid of makeup or any trace of femininity. She looked more like a man than a woman at a glance. She also wore a Chicago Cubs hat and Green Bay Packers socks pulled up to her knees.

"Hello," said the man-chick to Azriel.

Her breath smelled like milk and alcohol.

"You have this whole bar to sit at, and you sit next to me?" said Azriel. "Spread out."

"Well, yes," she said. She had an unrecognizable accent. "You see, I'm here to kill you, *Azrael*. And it's much easier to do it up close, wouldn't you agree?"

Azriel grinned.

He wasn't scared or nervous or even startled.

He expected someone would find him.

And that was okay.

After all, despite enjoying the peaceful life he had lived for nine months, he'd been aching for a fight the whole time.

To Be Continued...

ACKNOWLEDGMENTS

Normally I would put this at the front of the book. But some of the more eager-beaver readers might have given themselves a spoiler with a piece of information below. (I probably would.)

Anyway, first I must thank my editor and publisher Greg Perry. Without his encouragement and excitement for the material, I probably never would have written any fiction at all. His input and ideas made the book a lot better, too. Plus, Rood's background was strongly based on some teachings Greg has done about Christian pacifists and the connection between vegetarianism and violence.

I want to give another shout out to Jim Clair. A lot of Fezziwig's personality was thought out (and even acted out!) while we had dinner one night in Las Vegas. I knew we had hit on something because as we acted out the character at a dinner table of over a dozen people, the entire table was howling with laughter. So Jim, thanks man!

Can't forget Jodi Ardito, either. She has the patience of a saint. Especially when I'd space out during entire conversations thinking about the book's plot and characters, and ignoring whatever she was saying so I could jot down notes on my phone and email them to myself.

I'm also giving props to Guy Malone and Paradox Brown. The entire *King of Egypt* chapter was shamelessly based on research they did in a video called "The Case Against the First Book of Enoch." I highly suggest checking it out at www.ParadoxBrown.com.

Of course, I can't forget to mention the "Zombie Cop" fans who went out of their way to tell me how much they enjoyed it and demanded a sequel. If it weren't for them, I'd still be procrastinating. It'd take several pages to list everyone's names, but you know who you are. And, you have my gratitude.

Finally, I want to thank all the authors and moviemakers who created the stories that inspired me to write a book about vampires. Like "Lost Boys" and "Fright Night" and "'Salems Lot" and "Bram Stoker's Dracula" and the "Subspecies" movies (if you are a vampire fan and haven't seen them, you are simply missing out), and all the others that have influenced me over the years. Easter eggs about them are embedded throughout the book. Wonder if you caught them all...

Anyway, writing this book was a labor of love.

I hope you enjoyed reading it as much as I did writing it.

And if not?

Well, as Fezzwig would say, quit being such a faggot.

Ben Settle

54434241R00100

Made in the USA
Lexington, KY
16 August 2016